THE
BETRAYED

THE
BETRAYED

DEFEND THE CHILDREN AND PUNISH THE WRONGDOER

A NOVEL BY
KATE KRAY

Published by

MA✕CRIME

an imprint of John Blake Publishing Ltd,
3 Bramber Court, 2 Bramber Road,
London W14 9PB, England

www.johnblakepublishing.co.uk

First published in paperback 2010

ISBN: 978 1 84454 969 6

British Library Cataloguing-in-Publication Data:

A catalogue record for this book is available from the British Library.

Design by www.envydesign.co.uk

Printed and bound by CPI Group (UK) Ltd, Croydon, CR0 4YY

3 5 7 9 10 8 6 4

Papers used by John Blake Publishing are natural, recyclable products made from
wood grown in sustainable forests. The manufacturing processes conform to the
environmental regulations of the country of origin.

MA✕CRIME series commissioning editor: Maxim Jakubowski

In memory of
Pearl Thwaites

I would like to thank Maxine Penfold for the
compassion she showed Pearl while nursing her through
her final days.

I would like to thank:

John Wordsworth
Linda
Graham
Terry
Stevie
Mia
and, of course, Leo.

Kate Kray 2010

one

The London train emerged from the tunnel and gave a final sigh as it came to a halt at the platform. The heavy door swung open and Rosie stepped inside, praying that the decision that she had made was the right one. A whistle blew and the train lurched forward as it pulled away from the station and picked up speed until it reached its natural rhythm. Rosie swayed from side to side as she made her way along the narrow corridor, looking for somewhere to sit. Finding a near-empty carriage, she fell into a grimy seat, tossed down her bag, and settled back for the long return journey.

Her mind was racing as fast the Kentish countryside that flew past the window. She leaned over, wiped the condensation from the glass and peered out over the green fields outside. She had never really appreciated the beauty of the countryside as much as she did at that moment: the vivid burnt-amber, russet, and gold colours of the autumn leaves were spectacular. It was so beautiful, she almost began to forget about the harrowing day she'd just spent with Johnny.

Johnny was not happy. He wasn't happy at all. She had finally told him that she'd had enough – she wanted out. Johnny, as jealous and selfish as ever, had snarled at her, baring his teeth as he spat out a torrent of cruel words. They still rang in her ears... especially his parting shot: 'Friends won't go with you out of respect. Straight goers won't go near you through fear.'

She had tried to explain, as gently as she could, why she could no longer visit him in prison. For five, long, grinding years she had trudged around the country. Five years of waiting in the rain outside grey prison walls. Five years of bringing up their daughter, Ruby, on her own. And the situation wasn't about to change – Johnny was inside for 18 years. That meant it was left to Rosie to pay the hefty school fees, the mortgage, and all the other bills.

Watching her reflection in the train window, Rosie was horrified. She could almost see the life draining out of her, like someone had pulled a plug out from somewhere deep inside her. It was as if she was aging in fast forward: budding, flowering, blooming, then withering and dying. All before her very eyes.

She was still only 30, but she felt closer to 50... and probably even looked it, which was a bloody disaster when her career – or what remnants of a career she had – was reliant on her looks. Her dewy, porcelain-perfect complexion and sparkling emerald eyes had once featured in a series of make-up ads, and her dazzling white smile had, for a while, earned her a certain amount of success for its appearance in a toothpaste commercial. True, she'd achieved some success as an actress. Bit parts here and there, mostly. There was an episode of *Casualty*, a very brief stint in a minor sit-com, and a longer run in *EastEnders*… which is how she met Johnny Mullins. She had been introduced to him by a fellow actor at a glitzy party which Johnny was hosting with his brother, Eddie.

It had happened very quickly – too quickly, really. Like in the fairy stories she used to read as a little girl, Johnny, a knight in shining armour, had ridden into her life and carried her off, over the horizon into an world that she never knew existed. With his silk suits – hand-made in Savile Row, of course – and his Fratelli Rossetti, crocodile shoes, he was as smooth as butter and as slick as a whistle. He certainly had an aura about him; crowds seemed to melt away when he entered a room. When he approached, big, lumbering hard-men became suddenly light on their feet, stepping out of his way, and all the girls turned their heads. Still, Rosie couldn't quite put her finger on what exactly it was about him that attracted her. His reputation, perhaps? His awesome presence? Or could she put it down to an animal instinct, something she sensed? That alpha male, leader of the pack, top-dog aura. Whatever it was, there had been an instant attraction. You can call it what you will, but she called it love.

A relationship blossomed, and soon they were engaged. The wedding was an extravaganza, a spectacular of flounce and cash-waving. In the world that Johnny inhabited it was, without doubt, the wedding of the year.

The cream of the London underworld were there; gangsters from America flew over to pay their respects and enjoy a knees-up with their British counterparts.

It was a wedding reception with a difference, too. Only the very best was good enough: top London caterers, a bar stocked with every bottle imaginable, and cabaret acts were flown in from Vegas. Everyone was out to make a good impression, and, as the bride, Rosie knew that she would have to put on a bit of style. If there was ever a time for Versace, this was it. So she wore a beautiful, ivory-silk corset dress, decorated with thousands of Swarvoski crystals, with a train more than seven yards long. And, on her finger, a ring with 35 princess-cut diamonds.

An impressive range of Rollers, Bentleys, Mercedes, and a smattering of top-end sports cars, were parked bumper-to-bumper outside the country house where the reception was held. Hefty gangsters lumbered out of their mobile status-symbols, shrugging their broad shoulders and pulling at their lapels to free the high-living fat from their tight, starched-white collars. The dress code was as rigid as any society bash. All the men were kitted out the same: tailored suits, crisp white shirts, top pocket hankies, chunky 22-carat rings on their pinkies. All the girls had, quite obviously, been lying on sunbeds and sitting at the hairdressers with rollers in, after getting their roots done. At an occasion such as this, they wouldn't dream of arriving without the full works: high heels, dangly gold jewellery, lashings of lipstick, powder and paint. This was a wedding to be seen at.

A 300-strong army of guests slurped Cristal champagne and munched on canapés served on golden platters. Anyone who was anyone had turned out for the man himself, Johnny Mullins... and the new Mrs Mullins.

Over the following year, Johnny and Rosie's journey was full-on and in the fast lane: a new house in a fashionable part of Islington, a hedonistic lifestyle of clubs, money, fast cars, Cartier this, Gucci that...

She wanted for nothing and was swept off her feet by her new husband, much to the disapproval of her Aunt Madge. Over a cup of tea one Sunday, she warned Rosie: 'Watch him. His eyes are too close together.'

But Rosie had just laughed. She loved her auntie, but she didn't know Johnny like Rosie did. Besides, she enjoyed the attention and respect that came with being married to such a high-profile gangster. She was having a ball, the time of her life.

The only fly in the ointment, from her point of view, was Johnny's twin brother, Eddie; now, *his* eyes definitely *were* too close together. Eddie was as slippery as a box of frogs. He was so full of hate, like he had a great, gaping hole in the middle of his heart, and he could never inflict enough pain to fill it up. When Johnny and Eddie were together – which was most of the time – Johnny took on a different persona, one that could only be described as dangerous, intimidating, and all-out menacing. All they talked about was business, business, business... like it was all they lived for. Of course, Rosie never asked Johnny about what he did, and he never told her. It was an unspoken thing between them. 'So long as you got what you want, darling, that's all you need to know,' Johnny used to say, with a wink.

So that's how life settled down… with Johnny, Eddie, their best mate 'Hate-'em-all' Harry, and the rest of their firm – all big men in big suits who spoke mostly in whispers, out of the corners of their crooked mouths. Mondays, Tuesdays and Wednesdays were spent propping up the bar in the Tin Pan Club; Thursdays, Fridays and Saturdays in VIP lounges in fancy clubs Up West.

Aunt Madge was always telling Rosie that, 'Things that go up quickly, usually come down with a huge bump.' And boy, was she right. Within a few years of the wedding, Johnny was so high on success – and, above all else, cocaine – that their marriage went from bad to worse. His growing dependency soon began to wreak havoc on his finances, looks, and, most of all, his mood. If he didn't have his daily snort he would become angry, and, at times, even violent. It got progressively worse, until Johnny was frequently raising his hand to Rosie. It was becoming obvious that, under his gleaming armour, this knight was nothing more than a bullying, murdering thug. Soon, and so gradually that Rosie hardly noticed it, she had became totally under his control. Breaking away was simply not an option. Over the years, she had heard and witnessed things that nobody should have to experience, and she knew what he was capable of.

The only things that Johnny cared about was himself

and his bloody psycho brother, Eddie 'Mad Dog' Mullins. Rosie had become weary of the never-ending threats and ongoing violence, the uncertainty that came with living life on a knife edge. But, by that stage it hardly mattered what she thought, because it was perfectly clear that Johnny's cocaine habit had grown into a full-on addiction.

Johnny's behaviour and their exhausting home life took up much of Rosie's time, but what energy she had left she channelled into her acting. She managed to get a few auditions, but they came to nothing... until one day, much to her surprise, an amazing opportunity presented itself. It was on the day of her twentieth birthday; her agent rang to say that Andrew Brook-Fields, one of the nation's leading television producers, wanted to see her for a major new period drama.

'It's only for the lead!' said the agent. 'Kathy in *Wuthering Heights*. Great money, too.'

Rosie was ecstatic to finally have an opportunity to earn some money for herself – some 'straight money', instead of the tainted cash that her husband brought home. Johnny, on the other hand, was completely indifferent to the prospect of Rosie returning to her acting. He complained for a while about how he 'looked after her', but the truth was he was so lost in a haze of coke, that he rarely noticed anything that his wife said or did any more, and soon changed the topic of conversation.

Rosie put her heart and soul into the audition. She

wanted that part more than she wanted anything. The chance of a major part in a series was a wake-up call – it made her realise that, somewhere along the way, she had lost herself, lost her identity. She was sick and tired of being known as 'Mrs Rosie Mullins, wife of...'. She was never introduced as 'Rosie, the actress' any more, or even as 'Rosie, the person'. It was always 'Rosie, Johnny's wife'. She was fed up of the whole 'gangster' thing. She had to admit that, okay, it might have been glamorous and exciting at first, but now she longed for normality and respectability in her life.

During the brief, ten-minute audition she got the feeling that Andrew Brook-Fields was impressed with her, and her understanding of the part. The wait was unbearable, but finally the call from her agent came through... and her instincts had been right: she was first in line for the part! Rosie was over the moon, and she couldn't wait to tell Johnny her news. She so wanted him to be happy for her, to congratulate her, to make a fuss.

She should have known him by now. Johnny, being Johnny, was totally uninterested and just sneered at her when she told him the news. Like the selfish pig that he was, Johnny managed, in just a few, cruel words, to burst her bubble. Then the truth finally hit Rosie: all she was to him was something pretty that he could drape over his arm and show off, like a cashmere overcoat. Rosie's confidence was shattered by Johnny's reaction, and, after a truly disastrous second audition, the part of Kathy went to another girl.

Hot on the heels of this blow came more life-changing news: Rosie was four months pregnant. She was crushed, and resigned to her fate. So, with a heavy heart and an expanding waistline, she went back to being 'Rosie Mullins, wife of…'

The pregnancy did nothing to curb Johnny's behaviour, and his cocaine addiction grew, eating away at everything they had. The flash cars were the first to go, then the up-market house. They ended up in a two-up, two-down on Hewitt Way, just off the Roman Road in London's East End.

The day-to-day, week-to-week, month-to-month struggle went on. As the months rolled into years, things only got worse: endless police raids, violence, and constant domestic turmoil.

The only real joy in Rosie's life was their daughter, Ruby, who she adored. Rosie made a solemn promise to herself that she would never allow Ruby's father, with his addictions and violence, to drag them down with him. She managed to persuade Johnny, during a rare moment of harmony, to support the idea of sending their daughter to a private school; so, when she was six, they did just that.

But still, things between Rosie and Johnny weren't getting any better. The depths he sank to following a high became so harrowing that they were frightening to watch. Rosie frequently had to take Ruby to her Aunt Madge's, through fear of what he might do to her. He even threatened to murder Rosie on regular occasions… and she knew that he was more than capable of it. She had heard things; she had seen things. She was well aware that there was *nothing* Johnny wouldn't do, especially when he was coked up and flying high.

One terrifying night, during a particularly violent episode, he slapped Rosie to the floor, wrapped a giant hand around her neck, and held a gun to her head, screaming abuse. That was too much to take and Rosie, her eyes streaming with tears and with bruises darkening on her body, fetched a suitcase and started throwing clothes into it. But she knew in her heart that Johnny would never let her leave. Sure enough, moments later, he stormed into the bedroom, grabbed her by the arm, and swung her around to face him.

'*Nobody* leaves Johnny Mullins!' he spat, his eyes darting wildly, with a strand of thin saliva hanging from his snarling lips. 'I'll bury you in the woods first!'

Rosie was shaking uncontrollably – she had no choice. She had to stick it out. That night she wept for her lost life. It seemed that her remaining years were mapped out, that the nightmare would never end for her... or for Ruby.

Then, six months later, just when it seemed to Rosie that all hope was lost, fate played a hand: Johnny was arrested for drugs smuggling. It was a huge relief for Rosie. Out of the blue she had been given the chance of another life. In the days that followed, it felt like an enormous weight had been lifted off her shoulders. She didn't even consider that

Johnny's arrest could have a downside... but it did: Rosie's finances took a severe turn for the worse.

Rosie and Ruby started to rebuild their lives in the little terraced house on Hewitt Way. Ruby almost never mentioned her dad, and even pretended not to mind that he didn't write, and never used one of his precious phone cards to find out how they were coping. Life wasn't easy, and, at times, they had to really struggle to overcome the rising debts that threatened to engulf them.

The memories of her life with Johnny remained crystal clear in Rosie's mind, and this train journey was not the first time that she had been lost in them. She was snapped back to reality by squealing breaks as the train pulled into London's Charing Cross Station. She took a deep breath and tried to push any more thoughts of Johnny out of her mind as she stepped off into a small crowd of impatient travellers waiting to board.

The throng of people on the station concourse, bustling, pushing and shoving, made her head spin. She made her way through the sea of shuffling bodies to the road outside where irate drivers of black cabs hooted at red buses, which were blocking the cars, which were blocking the motorbikes, which, in turn, were blocking the pedestrians. She jumped on a No 40 bus, which would take her straight to the Roman Road.

After the slow bus ride home, and calling in at the corner shop for a pint of milk and a cut loaf, Rosie continued down the main road, past the dismal grey council estate where she had grown up. It was in one of these tower blocks, called Britley House, where her Aunt Madge had brought her up, and still lived today.

Rounding the corner into her terrace, where the houses were packed as tightly as sardines in a can, she headed towards home. She smiled a private smile as she approached the front door. It might be in need of a fresh lick of paint, she thought, but at least it's cosy and warm inside. Okay, it might not be as splendid as the posh Islington house that she had shared with Johnny, but it was not as grim as some. She glanced at her watch. Ruby wouldn't be back yet, it was still only six o'clock.

Rosie opened the front door and picked the dreaded mail up from the coconut fibres of the front-door mat – the postman, typically, hadn't been by the time she had left that morning. She went inside, the warmth of the snug, little sitting room wrapping itself around her like a big welcome hug.

After dropping her bag on the arm of the slightly tatty but comfy sofa that took up half the room, she threw her coat over the back of a chair and examined her post. The gas bill was paid, as was the electric, but she was nearly three months behind with her mortgage. *God, what else can I do?* thought Rosie. She was already working morning, noon and night trying to keep on top of the payments: an office cleaning job in the morning; Reception at the local doctor's surgery in the afternoon; and, in the evening, book-keeping at the Keyhole Club, a 'gentlemen's club' in Mayfair. Rosie shook her head as she walked into the kitchen, where she put away the bread and milk and dropped the brown envelopes on the counter top before unloading the washing machine.

Hearing a key in the front door, she looked up to see Ruby come bursting in, her cheeks flushed from the cold, and her long blonde hair whirling around her head. She was only 12, but looked more like 16. Ruby, of course, considered herself all grown up, more like 18.

'Hey Mum, you're home already!' she said, unceremoniously dumping her heavy school bag at the foot of the stairs, and unwinding her grey and purple scarf. 'How was Dad? Did you give him the elbow? What did he say? Bet he didn't like that. Oh, and guess who sent me a text today? Only Jake Gibson Blythe, oh my *God*, he's so cool. Actually he's so fit, everyone is crazy about him. Did you get my text about the trip to Switzerland?'

Rosie picked up the basket of wet laundry to carry it to the downstairs loo where they kept the tumble dryer.

'How much homework have you got?' she asked, trying to change the subject of the presumably expensive trip to Switzerland.

Ruby pulled open the fridge door and stood, examining its contents. 'Oh God, *tell* me about it, I've got this mega English project and maths coming out of my *ears*.' she moaned, selecting a stick of celery and taking a bite. 'Am I staying at Auntie Madge's tonight?'

'Yes, so go and grab what you need before we go. It's Friday night, fish and chip night. You know that.'

Ruby grabbed another stick of celery, her eyes sparkling

13

with mischief as she closed the fridge and turned to her mum.

'Friday – pension day! Fish and chips!' she said, taking another bite.

As Ruby squeezed past her, Rosie laughed, cupping her daughter's fresh face in her hands. 'Cheeky little monkey,' she said, feeling a powerful surge of love through her heart.

'What's up, Mum?' Ruby asked, looking up. 'Did Dad give you a hard time?'

'I'll be all right, chick,' she assured her, hoping she wouldn't mention the Switzerland trip again. Rosie told her to sort her things out while she went online to pay some bills. 'That's a good girl.'

Rosie sat at the old computer which stood in the corner of the sitting room on a scuffed and unstable desk. On the screen, staring back at her, was her bank balance – a big fat minus. Rosie's heart felt as heavy as lead.

'Mum, are you listening?' said Ruby, calling down to her.

'Yeah, yeah, yeah,' Rosie mumbled, as she waited for the computer to shut down. Ruby continued rambling on and on about her new crush, Jake Gibson Blythe.

'Mum, he is so fit… *so* fierce…' said Ruby, as she swept back into the room.

Rosie got up from the desk and looked at her daughter. She felt so guilty, knowing how disappointed Ruby would be when she told her that she couldn't afford to pay for the school trip. All of Ruby's friends were going, and she had talked of nothing else for weeks... no, *months*. Rosie had racked her brains, but still couldn't think of a way she could find the money for the trip, let alone the mortgage. She didn't want to disappoint Ruby, and, for a long time now she had avoided breaking the inevitable news. But she had to be told, and, Rosie knew, she couldn't put it off any longer.

'Rube, I've got to tell you something.'

'What?'

'I'm sorry,' she said softly, 'but I just haven't got the money for your Switzerland trip. I just can't afford it, darling... I'm so sorry.'

Ruby's eyes filled with tears. 'Mum, you *promised*! You said you would find the money. *Everyone* is going, and you said –'

'Rube, darling, I'm sorry,' said Rosie, turning her back so her daughter couldn't see the despair that she knew was etched on her face.

By now Ruby was crying, and when Ruby cried it was unlike anyone else had ever cried: she didn't get a red blotchy face, or a snotty nose... she cried little diamonds. Rosie just couldn't bear it.

'How much was it, five hundred?'

'Yeah,' said Ruby, between sobs, 'but we've already paid one hundred deposit, so I only need four more.'

Rosie took a deep breath and wiped the little diamonds from Ruby's eyes. 'Sweetie, don't cry,' she said. 'Look, I'll see what I can do, okay? Maybe I can get some extra shifts at the club. I got another letter about the house, so I've

15

got to sort that out... but I'll promise I'll try. You understand, don't you?'

Ruby's face softened, and she threw her arms around her mum and hugged her. 'Of course I do. Thanks, Mum.'

The drama was over.

'Oh and guess what?' said Ruby, sniffing and wiping the tears from her cheeks. 'Jake – you know, hunka-hunka Jake – he reckons I'm better looking than Lucy.'

'You're boy mad, you are,' Rosie said, with a smile. 'Come on, your fish and chip supper at Aunt Madge's will be getting cold. And I've got to get to the club by nine.'

two

'It's not her fault,' Rosie said, as Kristina drove them to Mayfair later that evening. 'She can't help wanting what all the other posh kids at her school have got. It's normal. It's just that I can't keep up with the endless school trips and uniforms... it costs a fortune.'

It was through Kristina that Rosie had landed her job at The Keyhole – but not as a nude waitress, like Kristina, or as a dancer. Rosie worked behind-the-scenes: a part-time office assistant, doing the books for Roberto Caesar, the flamboyant owner.

As the lights changed to green, Kristina drove across the Kings Road into Chaney Walk, where some of London's most expensive mansions were tucked away in private mews. Rosie vaguely registered them as they passed, aware that at least two of Ruby's schoolfriends lived in this part of town.

Not wishing to offend her, but unable to keep silent, Kristina finally said: 'You know the answer is in *your* hands, Rosie. No one will come knocking on your door offering you money. You have to make things happen yourself. You know Roberto would be more than happy for you to get out of that office... into the bar, or one of the private dining rooms.'

'Don't... don't...' Rosie said quickly, unwilling to even consider the possibility of waitressing topless, or, worse still, nude hostessing. But she knew, even as she fought with herself, that money was so tight that she couldn't afford to turn anything down. After all, Kristina did it every night.

'Don't get me wrong,' she said, after a deep breath, 'I'm not judging you for what you do, it's... it's just not for me.'

They'd had this conversation many times before and Kristina knew better than to push it. They were, after all, good friends.

'Tell you what,' said Kristina 'why don't you let me lend you the money then, for the trip. You can pay me back when you've got it. There's no rush.' She glanced over at Rosie. 'It wouldn't be a problem.'

'Thanks, but no thanks.' Rosie said, looking straight ahead. '"A friend in need is a pain in the arse", remember? If you borrow money from friends, that is the surest way to lose them. And I don't want to lose you as a friend.'

Kristina smiled. 'Well, the offer is there, if you change your mind.' She turned off the busy street, taking their regular short cut. 'And you're okay with the next school fees? When are they due?'

'Oh stop it! You're stressing me right out.'

'I'm only –'

'Just leave it... leave it, leave it. I don't want to talk about it any more.'

Rosie followed Kristina into the brightly lit hallway of the Keyhole Club, so called because rich, powerful, people pay hefty membership fees to be given their own front-door key. It's a spectacular, glamorous venue with numerous bars and private dining rooms, where anything and any fetish is catered for. Between six in the evening and three in the morning, London's most hardened partygoers are free to indulge themselves in almost any way they can imagine. There's the 'Wicked Dining Room', offering members an electric and occasionally painful entertainment; the 'Hard-On Room' for the naked gay orgies; the 'Rubber Room', with leather and latex uniforms; the 'Smack Room', where there is a spanking bench; and 'The Dungeons' where there are two St Andrew's crosses, a steel cage, and rope suspension.

'I'll come and see you when I've got a break, okay?' said Kristina, as she went off to get ready for the night's work. Rosie made her way upstairs to the office, where she found Roberto, the owner, sitting with his feet up on the desk, talking loudly into the phone. True to form he was wearing red, patent-leather shoes and electric-orange, silk socks to match his silk ruffled shirt.

Nobody did androgyny better than Roberto. He was, with his contoured cheeks, eclectic style, and shocking pink goatee beard, a genuine, flamboyant queen. Camp, loud, and popular, his playful, disarming persona had more than an approachable appeal. He was the ultimate host and everybody loved him. Rosie was no exception.

The moment he saw her enter, he slammed down the phone and jumped up.

'Rosie! Rosie! Rosie! My little angel!' he cried, enthusiastically. 'I'm *so* glad you're early! *Please*, you've got to help me out – one of the girls has phoned in sick. Please, I just need you to work in the club for *one* night. You don't have to do anything, just be there… and put on that *lovely* smile of yours.'

It was like a little ritual at the beginning of each shift: Roberto would say that Rosie was 'an angel', that she wasted in the office, and that she should go down and work in the club, 'where the *real* money is'. Her answer was always the same. But not tonight. Tonight was different. All Rosie could think about is how she was going to get the money for the mortgage and Ruby's trip. She knew it would break her daughter's heart if she couldn't go. Rosie stared over at Roberto, deep in thought.

'Okay then,' she said, finally.

'What?' Roberto eyes grew visibly wider.

'Okay… just for tonight.'

'Are you serious?'

'Just to help you out. But you'll have to show me what's what…. you know, the ropes.'

'Oh! You won't regret it,' he cried. 'And it's *nothing*. Just act. You're an actress, aren't you? All you have to do is make out you're "Luscious Lena the Hoochie Momma".'

Rosie smiled, and shook her head. 'Okay, Luscious Lena I am.'

Roberto clapped his hands together and jumped up and down, just like an excited child. 'Follow me,' he exclaimed, with a wave of his hand.

He led her downstairs to the dimly-lit bar and through to the dressing room reserved for the hostess girls. Kristina, wearing a transparent body stocking, her modesty barely preserved by a smattering of sequins, looked up quizzically as she saw her friend enter. She gave Rosie a reassuring smile as Roberto explained, then gave Rosie a hug, and her costume for the night.

Although she felt undeniably uncomfortable in her new role, Rosie shelved her morals for a few hours and got down to work. She kept reminding herself what Roberto had told her – that it was just like acting. Before she knew it, it was midnight, the club was packed, and the shows were already under way. Within the space of just three hours, even though she had consciously held back, she was surprised to see that she had earned almost £200 in tips.

And the money kept coming: by the end of the night, Rosie sat in the dressing room with £600 in front of her. She tucked it away in her bag and went to find Roberto. He was by the bar, submerged in darkness.

'Is it that time already?' he said, checking his watch. 'How time flies when you are enjoying yourself. Well, you've done a great job, my darling. It's just a pity you're not topping the bill *every* night.'

'Every night?' said Rosie, cocking her head and giving him a look. 'I told you, Roberto, this was a one-off. That's it. Done. One night only.' Inside, she felt a growing sense of shame.

'You sure?' said Roberto, raising his eyebrows. 'Oh, okay, I know… one night. I can see I'm wasting my breath.' Then, with an exaggerated look of disappointment, added 'Off you go, then. See you tomorrow.'

'See you.'

'And Rosie, thanks again for helping me out, okay? I really appreciate it.'

Sitting in the mini-cab on the way home Rosie stared blankly out at the passing streets. It was dark and dank, drizzling with that fine rain she hated so much. Although what happened at the club wasn't as bad as she had feared, she couldn't shake off the feeling that she'd let herself down. She felt cold inside, tainted by some of the things she had just witnessed. She hoped that most of the events of the evening would soon fade from her memory… especially the awkward 20 minutes or so when that businessman had tried to persuade her to 'accompany' him to his hotel. *Has it come to this?* she asked herself. She consoled herself by switching her thoughts to Ruby – and how she was going to break the news that she could afford the trip, after all. They could even go shopping on Saturday, with all that money. But, try as she might, Rosie couldn't get rid of the grimy, cold feeling in the depths of her stomach. And she knew what that feeling was: she was ashamed of herself.

Once she was home, she ran a bath to help her relax. Those exotic oils that Aunt Madge had given her for Christmas, she thought, might make her feel clean again. Sitting on the edge of the bath, wrapped in a white fluffy towel, she watching the red oil swirl around in the steaming water. Eyes heavy with fatigue, heart heavy with shame, Rosie put her head in her hands and wept.

three

L ate the next morning, the red light on her
answerphone blinked a summons. Rosie, her eyelids
still heavy from the night before, reached out and hit the
playback button. *Please, no more bad news*, she said to
herself, as the first message began to play.

To her relief it was her acting agent, Annie: 'Hi, hun!'
she chirped, 'Can you give me a buzz as soon as you get
this. It's a bit last minute, but there's something come up.
As soon as you get this, okay? 'Bye.'

The answerphone announced '*Message 2*'. Rosie
recognised the voice immediately. 'Hey Rosie, it's me,
Stevie. I'll be in London next week. Can you and Ruby-
two-shoes meet me at Mum's? I'll treat you both to
lunch. I've got some great news. Gotta run, sweetie. As
they say in the USA, have a nice day!'

Rosie tapped the button, turning the machine off. The
sound of Stevie's voice had stopped her in her tracks,
washed over her in a wave of nostalgia, making Rosie
feel sort of happy and sad and the same time. God, she

missed Stevie... 'Stephanie' to everyone else, but always 'Stevie' to her.

Stevie was more like a sister to Rosie than a cousin. They had been brought up together by Auntie Madge after Rosie's mother and father had been killed in a car accident. The two girls had slept in the same bed in a cramped bedroom in the grimy high-rise block of flats, and that sense of closeness had never disappeared.

Like Rosie, Stevie had survived an abusive relationship. Her ex-husband had a real darkness in him, and he had knocked poor Stevie from pillar to post. After a long, frank discussion with Rosie, Stevie had left him and moved back in with Auntie Madge... but, as it turned out, she didn't stay for long. One night she borrowed Rosie's most sexy dress and went to an exclusive night club in Soho. There she got talking to Joe, a well-heeled American professor who had worked at Harvard University. Joe was rich, handsome; he had it all. It was love at first sight and within two months Stevie had packed up and moved to Sarasota-Bradenton, on the west coast of Florida. It *must* have been love, Rosie thought at the time, as there's no other reason Stevie would have left behind her beloved Shih-Tzu dog, Dibble, for Aunt Madge to look after. Even though that dog was the psycho dog from hell, it was a living, yapping reminder of her friend in Florida – so Rosie was always pleased to see it. Aunt Madge idolised that animal, and wouldn't have a bad word said against it, no matter how it behaved.

Within seven months of moving to the States, Stevie had a whopping great diamond engagement ring sparkling on her finger; and within a year she was an all-American bride... with breast implants, hair extensions, the works.

Of course, Rosie was happy for her friend but when Stevie had left for America it broke her heart. And Ruby was distraught, too, missing her godmother deeply. Sure, they kept in touch by email and the odd phone call, but it wasn't the same as having her round the corner. So, the prospect of seeing her in just a week put a huge smile on Rosie's face.

She grabbed her mobile and sent Stevie a quick text: 'yes please!!!xxx'. After pressing 'send', Rosie looked up to see the light on the answerphone light still flashing. She pressed 'play' again, and the smile on her face was instantly replaced by a look of sheer terror.

'Hello, Rosie.'

The blood in her veins was suddenly turned to ice. The gruff, menacing, and familiar voice on the machine stung at her ears like a trapped wasp.

'So you think that's it, do you? That you can just walk away like that? Nobody leaves Johnny Mullins... *nobody*. You understand?' She could hear Johnny take a deep, rasping gulp of air, before he continued. 'A friend of mine – a big fella he is – will be out on home leave soon. I told him about you, what you've done to me. And you know what? He wasn't too happy. Oh, no. He said he might come round and say hello. Not sure when he'll be able to pop round and see you, but he'll come all right. Look after yourself.'

'*End of message,*' came the robotic voice from the machine. '*To listen to the message again, press –*'

Rosie hit the button and backed away. Her heart was beating so fast it felt like it could explode. She knew the nastiness was coming – she'd been married to Johnny long enough to know that there would be repercussions for breaking it off with him – but *this*? Setting one of his heavies on her? She hadn't, in her darkest nightmares, expected that.

Rosie took a deep breath and collapsed, shaking, into a chair. Inside her head, through the mist of fear, came a voice, strong and resolute. She was not going to let Johnny, or any of his so-called friends, get to her. She was going to be strong, for Ruby's sake. She was going to move on with her life. Step one, she was going to get up, and return her agent's call.

'Annie, its Rosie.' Her voice was still shaking.

'Rosie, where have you been?' Annie said. 'I'm sorry, but you've missed the boat now…'

'What?'

'Channel 4 was holding auditions for this sit-com early this morning and wanted to see you for it. You should have called last night, darling. I assumed you weren't interested.'

Rosie mumbled some excuse about being ill, and put the phone down. Her head was spinning. *This is just what I need…* Deciding not to dwell on things, Rosie set up the ironing board. She wanted to get through at least half the pile before she went to pick up Ruby.

Ruby let out a jubilant cry when Rosie handed her a cheque for the remaining £400 she needed for the Switzerland trip. She hugged her daughter, gripping her in a tight bear-hug, and told her they were going shopping for some 'retail therapy'. If felt good, spoiling Ruby, for once. Dear sweet Rube – she never complained about not having as much as the other girls at her school, or that her school blazer was worn, or that she was wearing last season's fashions. *Bless her.* Ruby always made do, and never grumbled. And, God knows, Rosie needed to do something to take her mind off things.

As they wandered around the shops, helping Ruby pick out some new outfits to impress her latest crush, Rosie knew that what money she had left from her sordid night at the Keyhole was not going to last long… it certainly wouldn't fill the gaping hole in her mortgage payments. And what would happen if they needed to get away for a few weeks, until the situation with Johnny had died down? With things the way they were, they just didn't have that luxury.

Rosie wrestled with her conscience about doing another night at the club and, although she had sworn to herself just the night before that she would never to do that again, she knew, in her heart, that it made sense. One more night, just *one* more shift at the club – if she really went for it – would enable her to pay enough of the mortgage to keep them off her back for a few months. She had to get herself straight and sort out their money worries… in the short term, at least. Could she face another night at the Keyhole? *Just one more night?* After all, she told herself, it wasn't real. It was only acting. It was her alter ego, 'Luscious Lena the Hoochie Momma'. As she stood in the queue with Ruby, waiting to pay for a new pink top, she made the decision to do one more shift.

So, that evening Rosie found herself back in the club, working the floor. She steeled herself before greeting the first arrivals: four Arabs, over from Dubai for a three-day conference, and one smartly-suited businessman.

Rosie waited for them to sign in, then escorted them to the Foxy Dining Rooms. A drop-dead sexy Polish girl, by the name of Ola, opened the door dressed as a sly fox.

With a lick of her lips, and a swish of her bushy tail, she purred, 'Good evening, gentlemen.'

By 12.30 the Keyhole Club was buzzing. It was hectic and, Rosie thought, much busier than the previous night. Nearly all of the private dining rooms were occupied, with the parties in full swing. Rosie went over to Reception and didn't have to wait long for the next punter to arrive. A large, thespian-looking man, his face almost totally obscured by his wide-brimmed hat, signed himself in. Obviously a regular, he walked right up to Rosie and, with a dramatic and exaggerated wave of his hand, theatrically demanded, 'Take me to the Hard-On Room!'

The Hard-On Room was a magnet for gay men from every walk of life. If you have the compulsion – and more importantly, the money – then anything goes. It was, for a certain sector of society, an extremely fashionable, fun and funky place to spend an evening. With its contemporary, subterranean feel, and live stage acts, it was always busy.

Rosie ushered the man and his enormous hat into the room and saw that tonight was no exception, it was packed. Strewn around the plush interior, like disregarded, damp towels on a bathroom floor, lay half-naked men, ogling the special stage act. Rosie averted her eyes as she led the excited toff to the bar for a glass of champagne. The bar was four-deep with flouncing revellers, with handsome young men in leather thongs, serving the vastly over-priced champagne to rich closet queens. A handsome, dark-skinned, twenty-something Adonis, Mikey – one of the regular club boys – handed a glass of champers to the man in the hat, who then disappeared off to watch the action on the stage.

'How's the new job?' said Mikey, flashing a pearly grin.

'Don't *you* start,' Rosie said, half-shouting over the blaring music. 'This is my last night, so make the most of it.'

'Do me a favour, Rosie darling,' said Mikey, nodding over at the end of the bar. 'Take that bottle of Cristal to booth number five. I'm run off my feet here.'

Rosie gave him a wink and took the tray, with the champagne and four, tall-stemmed glasses, and made her way down the dimly lit corridor to the booth. She paused for a moment at the door, and reminded herself that whatever she felt about what was going on inside, she mustn't let it show on her face.

'Champagne' she called, knocking gently at the door.

After knocking again, there was still no reply, so she eased the door open, being careful not to upset the tray. On entering, despite her little pep talk, Rosie couldn't stop a gasp from escaping. It was a sight so shocking, even by the standards of the Keyhole Club, that she felt the blood drain from her cheeks.

In the room were five men. She recognised one of them instantly – Pascal, one of the pretty boys who worked at the club. He was no more than a boy, really. Eighteen, maybe nineteen. He had a ball strapped in his mouth, and his eyes were wide with pain and fear.

One of the other men was holding Pascal's arms, two others held his legs outstretched, while the fourth man, who was stripped to the waist, was having his fun. The floor was littered with empty bottles and a variety of sick sex toys. And, on the mirrored table were thick lines of cocaine, rolled up bank notes… and a hat. A familiar hat, in fact. A leather, pork pie hat which Rosie instantly recognised as the exact same sort of hat that Hate-'em-all-Harry always wore.

If the hat was all that Rosie had seen, she might have left the booth and dismissed it as a coincidence. But then she noticed something else. The man with his back to her, having his fun, had a large Celtic cross tattooed on his massive, hairy back. Johnny had the exact same Celtic cross – with 'Eddie' written underneath it – on *his* back. Rosie had often thought it was a shame that Johnny had chosen to have the name of his psychotic twin-brother needled into his flesh.

A voice inside Rosie was screaming at her to get out of the booth, but curiosity got the better of her. She leaned forward and, peering into the dim light, she saw, tattooed under the Celtic cross, one word: 'Johnny'.

There was no doubt. It was Eddie, her own brother-in-law, Johnny's twin. Quietly, and as quickly as she could, Rosie placed the champagne on a side table and left, mentally praying that none of the men would look up as she left. She held her breath until she gently closed the door behind her.

Rosie was in total shock. She couldn't make sense of what she had witnessed. *How could this be?* Eddie was married to his posh wife, Sylvia. Their two daughters were in an expensive school. And they had an elegant, expensive house in Millionaire's Row in St John's Wood. *The ideal home! The perfect marriage!* What the hell was Eddie doing?

As she made her way back to the Reception, Rosie's mind was racing. A million questions rushed through her brain. She knew that she had to compose herself, try to think straight and act normal.

First off, she knew that she couldn't risk bumping into Eddie or any of his friends. She found Roberto near the entrance, and told him that she'd spotted an old schoolfriend and didn't want to embarrass him. Could she avoid Reception and the Hard-On Room for the rest of the night? Roberto smiled and replied that she could work wherever she liked.

Rosie kept a relatively low profile in the Smack Room

until the Keyhole closed. Kristina had stayed on until the end, too, so she gave her a lift home. During the journey back through the dark, dank streets, they sat in virtual silence. Rosie's head was spinning. She glanced over at Kristina. She so wanted to say something, to share what she had witnessed in booth number five, but she couldn't find the right words.

Before she knew it, they were outside her house. Kristina leaned over and kissed Rosie goodnight.

'You okay?' she asked.

'I'm just tired. Thanks for the lift,' said Rosie.

'Any time. See you,' Kristina said, pulling the car door shut and giving her a wave through the window before driving off.

Rosie shivered. It was a cold, autumn night. The rain was coming down in buckets, and the air smelt of wet leaves. She pulled her coat collar and ducked her head to guard against the chill wind as she scurried up the garden path, fumbling for her front door keys.

Once inside, she headed straight for the kitchen and put the kettle on, to make herself some tea. As she waited for the water to boil she sat at the table with her head in her hands, knees pressed tightly together. Her eyes were heavy with fatigue. There were no real thoughts in her head, only vague whispers of what needed to be done tomorrow... or today, as it already was. She tried to push the image of what she had seen in the club to the back of her mind. She had to focus on *her* life.

She counted the money from the club. *Only £470?*

How can it be worse than last night? The mortgage payments would eat up all of that money in a flash and still be hungry for more. She made the tea, trying to forget about it all. It was a desperate situation. Even if she worked a hundred shifts at the club, she still had no idea how she was going to deal with Johnny's threats.

She went over to the sink and poured away the remaining half of her tea. Right now, she was just so tired, so exhausted, she just needed to sleep. Wearily she made her way up the stairs and tried to convince herself that she would be better able to deal with her problems tomorrow.

four

It was lunchtime when Rosie finally got out of bed. After tipping a can of tomato soup into a saucepan and putting it on to heat, she switched on the computer, intending to look for a new job. The night before had made it obvious that she was just not suited to that sort of work. Surely she'd find *something* she could do... something to replace her income from the club.

She got as far as the Google homepage when her phone started ringing. She jumped up, lowered the gas on the stove, and grabbed the receiver.

'Hello, Rosie Mullins speaking.'

'Oh, I'm so glad it's you, I was afraid I might get the answerphone, again,' said the voice at the other end. 'How are you?' Realising who it was, Rosie was hit by a powerful wave of emotion.

'Stevie!' she gasped. 'Oh my God! It's so wonderful to hear you! How are you? I'm sorry I haven't called but... but... '

'Don't worry, we've both been busy and emails are fine… up to a point. I needed to hear your voice, though, and to see you.'

'You mean you're coming over?' said Rosie. At that moment, she could hardly imagine anything better.

'Actually, it means if you go to the front room window and take a peek, I am standing right outside.'

Rosie's heart contracted as a deluge of tears surged into her eyes. Without wasting another moment, she ran across the sitting room and tore open the door, almost afraid that she was dreaming.

Stevie was standing there with open arms.

'Oh my God… my God,' she sobbed. 'You don't know how happy I am to see you!'

'Wow… you look it,' Stevie grinned.

Stevie looked incredible. Her auburn hair was long and sleek; her make-up applied perfectly; the rest of her was all wrapped up in winter furs and long leather boots. She was as slender and elegant as the ideal American housewife. In their day, they had been quite a twosome, but Rosie was under no illusions about who the real beauty was – Stevie was in a class of her own.

'When did you get back to England?' Rosie demanded, holding her cousin at arm's length to get a good look at her. 'And why didn't you tell me you were coming?'

'It was all rather last minute. I was going to send you an email, and then I took it into my head to surprise you.'

'Well you certainly have,' Rosie assured her, cupping Stevie's beloved face in her hands.

'Look at you! You're more gorgeous than ever. So sophisticated. So… so… *Americanised.*'

Stevie stared back, her warm eyes filled with love, and with a growing smile on her face.

'I'm as English as black cabs, double-decker buses, and red telephone boxes,' she laughed. 'And I'm *freezing*. Any chance of a cuppa? Or, if you fancy it, we could crack open a bottle of champagne.'

'I'm sorry, I'm all out of champagne,' said Rosie, as they went inside.

Stevie swung a large Louis Vuitton bag from off her shoulder and pulled out a bottle of Bollinger. 'You surely don't think I've come empty handed!'

'Let me take your fur coat,' said Rosie, closing the door. 'It's amazing. Did you get it in the States?'

'I did. And if you like it, you can have it.'

Rosie's eyes narrowed. 'Oh no, I didn't mean that.'

'I know you didn't, but I have another one almost the same. So consider that one an early birthday present, or belated, or whatever,' said Stevie. She pressed the bottle of champagne against the back of her hand. 'I'm afraid this isn't as cold as it should be, but it will have to do. Glasses in the same place?'

Laughing and hugging the fur coat, Rosie watched her cousin sail into the kitchen, where she carried on like she had never been away.

'When did you get here?' Rosie asked, following her. 'And where are you staying?'

'I arrived at the crack of dawn this morning,' she replied. 'I'm staying at the Ritz.'

Stevie's eyes were dancing as she popped the cork off the champagne bottle. She grinned and, after filling two glasses, handed one to Rosie.

'Cheers! my dear. Here's to you.'

Rosie smiled as they clinked glasses. Normally she wouldn't have a drink so early in the day... especially when she had to go to work in an hour. *What the hell*, she thought, knocking it back. No sooner had she put her glass down, Stevie grabbed the bottle for a refill.

'You took a risk coming unannounced,' Rosie told her, as the champagne fizzed over her fingers.

'Confession number one: I have just come from Mum's, and she told me you'd be in.' Rosie's eyes narrowed slightly. Stevie continued, 'She also brought me up to speed with everything that's been happening with you, which doesn't seem to have made your emails.' Rosie's frown deepened. 'Why on earth didn't you tell me you have been finding things so hard? You know very well I would've helped you out.'

'Whatever Aunt Madge has told you, she's exaggerating,' Rosie said, defiantly. 'Anyway, I sure as hell wasn't going to fill my emails with sob stories, especially with you and Joe getting on so well. I've got my pride, you know.' At that very moment she remembered how, last night, what little pride she had left she had shed along with her clothes at the Keyhole Club. Her spark faded. 'Actually, I'm not sure if I *do* have my pride,' she mumbled. 'But don't let's go into that.'

'No, let's,' Stevie insisted, pulling out a chair, and sitting at the table. 'But before we go any further, you are going to let me give you the money for Ruby's school trip.'

'Aunt Madge had no business telling you about that,' said Rosie, in a flash. 'Anyway, it's not a problem.'

'Of course Mum was right to tell me!' said Stevie. 'Ruby's my *goddaughter*. It's my responsibility to help you out. So don't argue. I haven't forgotten the time you bailed *me* out, when I was broke, and you and Johnny were flush. Over a hundred quid, as I recall. It's all relative and, anyway, as your best friend, I'm not going to let you dig yourself into a hole that you can't get out of. The boot's on the other foot now. It's my turn to help you out… and, more to the point, I *want* to help.' She took a sip of her drink before adding, in a quiet voice, 'If you can't rely on your family, then who can you rely on?'

'I think I'm already in the hole,' said Rosie, not sure whether she wanted to laugh or cry. 'Not that I can't get out of it, but I…' Her voice trailed off as, once again, she remembered the night before and what she had done.

'What is it?'

Even though she could talk to Stevie about anything, the words just wouldn't come.

'Come on, nothing's that bad,' Stevie prompted. 'You know me, I've been around the block a couple of times. I've heard it all… seen it, done it. In fact, I've probably got the t-shirt somewhere.'

Rosie's smile was fading. She stared at the floor. Her throat felt constricted and dry. She knew that once the words were out, it would, somehow, be more real, and she would have to face up to what had happened.

'Last week,' she began, staring at her drink, as if the words were hiding there at the bottom of the glass, 'Ruby and I had a row and ...' She shook her head. 'Well, not exactly a row... it's just... the mortgage, the bills, the school fees, you know. Then, to top it all, this school trip came up. It was just the straw that broke the camel's back. I tried to explain to Ruby that we couldn't afford it. She got upset, and we had a... heated debate. I suppose it doesn't have anything to do with Ruby, actually.'

Rosie took a deep breath and tried again.

'An opportunity to earn good money – well, easy money – has been there for a while. The other girls do it... well, it's their job. They know the score, and what's expected of them. They're fine with it.' Looking up from her drink, Rosie saw her friend looking back, her eyes sympathetically urging her to continue. 'Oh Stevie, am I rambling? I don't know. I'm sorry.'

'Can I take it that you're talking about the Keyhole?' said Stevie.

Rosie nodded, then blurted out, 'So I did it. Last Friday. I guess I hit rock bottom. I don't really know what was going through my head... I lost my mind. I had this feeling that my world was collapsing around me, like a pack of cards, and if I could just *do* something then and there, right away, to make some money, it would make it better. And if that's not enough, I told Johnny that I didn't want to be with him any more –'

'About time. Good on you,' Stevie muttered, quick as a flash.

'He was angry,' Rosie continued. 'Bloody livid, he was. He's even threatened to set one of his heavies on me. I got these phone calls. Oh, Stevie, I'm so tired. I'm… I'm sick of trying. I work so hard, and still I've got nothing.'

Rosie took a long, unsteady breath, swallowing hard. Her hands were locked together so tightly that her nails were cutting into her palms.

'And?'

'The answer was right there in front of me. It wasn't even that difficult in the end, all I had to do was act. It didn't have to be *me*. It was… "Luscious Lena the Hoochie Momma".' Rosie made a sound something between a laugh and a sob. 'It was someone else who went into the private dining room, carrying food and drinks to a bunch of drunken toffs.

'I became this other person – so when they grabbed me, I just giggled and squirmed, because that's what Luscious Lena would do.

'I earned good tips, enough to pay for Ruby's trip, anyway. But I knew, deep down, that it wasn't me. This one man – horrible, he was – offered me two thousand pounds if I'd go back to his hotel room for the night… It seemed like so much money and I knew, if I could just stay as Luscious Lena… But I felt like a part of me was rotting inside me. My mask was slipping, you know? Cracks were starting to appear. I just wanted to get out of there. It was bad enough – what I *had* done – and, when

41

I found myself even considering this man's offer, I felt like this alter ego might take over. Like next time she *would* go to the hotel room. It was horrible.'

Rosie had thought that sharing this would make her feel better, but, looking at her friend, all she felt was misery and shame.

'That's how low I've sunk' she mumbled, attempting a smile. 'That's how I'm using all that drama training, all those hours that I spent learning how to act, working hard trying to be the best actress I possibly could. Here I am, hiding behind an ugly mask, trying to –'

'Stop! Stop!' Stevie broke in. 'Goodness me! Rosie, Rosie, listen to yourself! Anyone would think you had been working street corners or something, or committed some terrible, heinous crime. All you did was let a few blokes see your wobbly bits! Darling, it happens all the time – on beaches, in magazines…'

'But I let them *touch* me.'

Stevie rolled her eyes, and proclaimed sarcastically, 'Well, let's take you directly to the gallows and hang you! Or do you want me to drag you off to the market square, put you in the stocks, and start chucking rotten tomatoes?' She reached over and squeezed Rosie's hand. 'Come on! Get real. We've *all* done things that we've regretted the next morning. A few blokes grabbing your boobs is pretty low down the scale.'

'It may be to you!' Rosie exclaimed. 'But for me it was like I had crossed some invisible line.'

It was all too much, and she burst into tears. Stevie

put down her drink, and wrapped her up in a reassuring bear hug.

'Okay,' she whispered, 'I get the picture. It's not who you are or what you wanted to do. I'm just trying to put it into some kind of perspective. You did what you had to do to keep the wolf from the door, like anyone else would have done. You've got to remember, when it came right down to it, you *didn't* go back to that hotel room. You're still you, huh?'

'But, next time, I *might*. That's what scares me.'

'Well, there won't be a next time, will there,' said Stevie, handing Rosie her drink. 'Look how it's made you feel. No, no more – it's done, finished. Just put it behind you. Come on, you know what I think?'

'What?' said Rosie, her breathing finally returning to normal.

'All right, it wasn't a great experience, but you've had worse. I *know* you, Rosie. I think that that you're focusing all of your energy on what happened at the Keyhole, and not telling me what the real problem is.' She topped up their drinks before asking the question: 'What happened with Johnny?'

Rosie stopped dead. Yes, *what about Johnny?* She took a long drink before she began to speak.

'I went to see him, down in Maidstone, and I told him that it was over. It's been five years of prison visits... and for what? It's not like the marriage was working on the outside, so I don't know what I was trying to achieve.'

'Well, it was for Ruby, wasn't it?'

'Yeah. He loves her… in his own way. But that's not a good enough reason to carry on. I've had a gutful of his demands. "Do this", "do that". He thinks that a two-hour visit is just that, but it's not. It's all day, travelling there and back, to whatever desolate prison he's in.

'Then when I finally make it to the visit, he barks orders at me. "Get me this", "get me that". And then he wonders why I don't bring Ruby! It's all about Johnny and *his* needs, and to hell with anyone else. And for what? Like it's going to be roses when he gets out? Whatever happens, I know I just don't want that life anymore.'

Rosie stared out of the window at the rain that had started to drum a gentle beat against the window. 'But you know what they're all like. They can't let it go. And that phone call scared me half to death. Johnny's capable of anything. I just don't know what to expect. I knew who he was when I married him, so it's my own stupid fault, I suppose. But I just can't *take* it any more, I really can't, Stevie.'

Stevie leaned back in her chair and thought for a moment. 'Oooh, now, getting away from Johnny – that is a biggie. But where there's a will, there's a way.'

'There was something else at the club, Stevie.'

'Come on!' said Stevie, exasperated. 'Focus, girl!'

'No, something I saw. Something that I wasn't going to tell anyone.'

'Look,' exclaimed Stevie, throwing her arms in the air. 'I know lots of horrible stuff goes on there, but let's –'

'No,' Rosie snapped loudly, cutting her off.

'Something… to do with Johnny. It's a bit… well, complicated. It could seriously kick things off.'

Stevie's ears pricked up. 'Do tell.'

Lowering her voice, Rosie continued, 'Well, you won't believe this, but Eddie was at the club last night –'

'Eddie?'

'Yeah. I saw him… with one of the young boys there. I saw him but he didn't see me.'

Stevie laughed a belly laugh. 'You mean, *with* a boy?'

'Yeah, this young lad, Pascal, who works there.'

'You are *joking*. But he's married to Sylvia. The dirty swine!' Stevie sunk back into her chair. 'Bingo… got him, bang to rights.'

'Honestly? I wish I hadn't seen it.'

'What are talking about!' Stevie said, jumping up, and pacing. 'We'll blackmail Eddie. They'll *have* to leave you alone. Johnny will start paying maintenance again – how long has that been? Four years?'

'You know what they're like! That's a dangerous game.'

'You've got to fight fire with fire!' said Stevie, turning to Rosie. 'We'll be as devious as that creep is. After all, can you imagine if Sylvia found out? All of his golfing bods? Eddie would be *mortified*.

'Can you imagine?'

'Are you sure he didn't see you?

Rosie nodded. 'I'm sure.'

'So that's sorted then!' said Stevie, bringing her hands together with a loud clap. 'We'll blackmail Eddie – he'll stop grassing your every movement to Johnny. They'll call off their hounds. You'll get support, Ruby will be sorted, and you'll live happily every after.'

As a plan, it sounded perfect. But Rosie had made plans before, and she knew that, however simple they seemed in theory, they had a habit of going badly wrong in practice. Not that Stevie seemed to be worried. She poured the last drops of the champagne and gave Rosie a wink.

'Okay, sweetie? Stevie's home now, so *everything* will be fine. Now, drink up.'

five

The menswear department in Harrods wasn't Rosie's usual stomping ground, but Pascal had told her he needed to buy a new outfit, and insisted that they should meet there.

Pascal was a boy in a hurry, a boy who was looking for action. He oozed confidence –

a young man with places to go and people to see. He was, as he frequently reminded everyone, 'the next Jean-Claude Van Damme', and was only working at the Keyhole until his acting career took off. When he wasn't doing a shift in the Hard-On Room, he was busy reading scripts, pestering agents, or working out at the gym. Not that he was ever short of shifts, mind. Roberto, the owner, had a real soft spot for Pascal, and Rosie had frequently heard about them 'sharing a cab' at the end of the night.

Rosie spotted him the moment she walked in. He was standing in front of a mirror, holding up a shirt and carefully examining himself. A pair of hungry-looking female assistants faffed around him, ogling every inch of his toned body. With his French accent and good looks, Pascal had real sex appeal… and he knew it. He wasn't shy of encouraging anyone, and women were always falling for him. Unfortunately for them, of course, he was a confirmed homosexual.

He tossed the shirt aside and began fingering his way along the Armani clothes section, periodically holding up different garments, with his attentive assistants in tow. Rosie was not immune to his charm, and she had warmed to Pascal the moment she had met him. They had struck up a friendship when he had asked to borrow her lip gloss, of all things.

Spotting her, Pascal held out his hands, offering a warm embrace.

'Bonjour, Rosie!' he said, kissing her gently on both cheeks.

'Bonjour!'

'Tell me,' he asked, holding up a denim jacket by Armani, 'does this blue complement my eyes?'

Rosie confirmed that it did, a sentiment quickly echoed by the sales assistants.

'Haven't you enough designer labels?'

'Calvin Klein, Yves St Lauren, Gucci… a boy can never have enough!' he announced, tossing the jacket over to one of the assistants.

Rosie took Pascal by the beautifully manicured hand, and began to lead him away from the racks of clothes and towards the food hall.

'Come on,' she said. 'Let's go have something to eat.'

As they ate their bacon-and-avocado club sandwiches, Pascal asked, 'So, *ma chérie*? What can I do for you?'

Rosie opened her mouth, and closed it again. This was going to be harder than she had expected.

'I need to ask you about something… well, some *one* actually.'

Pascal cocked his head to one side, a puzzled look on his face.

'Who, Rosie? What person?'

Rosie explained, slightly embarrassed as she did, how she had worked a few waitressing shifts, and had seen Pascal in the booth number five the other night. Pascal shrugged, and took an enormous bite of his sandwich. Rosie could tell that, behind the mask, he was a little uncomfortable.

'You know the man with the cross tattoo on his back?'

'Johnny, his name is.'

'No, that's the name tattooed on his back, all right. But Johnny is his brother. His name is Eddie.'

'Well, Johnny, Eddie, whatever. They just call him "Mad Dog",' his accent sounding suddenly much stronger.

'Yeah, Mad Dog Eddie. That's him.'

'And he *is* a dog. Very, very nasty man. A bad man. He disrespect me.' Pascal burnt up a lot of energy even when he was chatting – his hands and face expressing as much as the words that came from this mouth. Rosie could tell that his hatred of Eddie was genuine, deep. Although she took no pleasure in seeing Pascal get hot under the collar, she knew it would make him sympathetic to his cause.

49

'You still hungry? Another sandwich?'

'Why not?' answered Pascal, quick as a flash.

After Rosie called the waitress over and placed the order, Pascal gave her a charming smile and asked, concerned, 'Why are you interested in the Mad Dog?'

'It's a long story.'

'Don't get involved with him, okay? He is a dangerous man.'

'I know that, don't I?' said Rosie. 'He's my brother-in-law.'

She went on to disclose to Pascal the whole unsavoury saga: her marriage to Johnny, Eddie's murderous past, and the fall-out from telling Johnny that it was over.

'So I need something I can use against them. You know what I'm talking about, don't you?'

'The "security" tapes?'

'Exactly.'

It was one of the Keyhole's many secrets: Roberto videotaped everything that happened in the booths of the Hard-on rooms. Whether it was for security, Roberto's own personal gratification, or simply for salacious secrets that he could sell to a Sunday newspaper on a rainy day, nobody knew. Rosie had hardly been able to believe it when Kristina had told her about the hidden cameras that she'd found.

'Eddie has a lot to lose,' Rosie explained to Pascal. 'A house, a family… not to mention his reputation. Sylvia – that's his wife – would take him for everything he's got, if she found out about this.'

'Clever girl, Rosie. You have seen the cameras when you work in the office, yes?'

'Yes. But I also know that Roberto takes the week's tapes away somewhere every Sunday. Look,' she said, lowering her voice, 'I know you and Roberto are close, so I was wondering if you knew where he takes them?'

Pascal thought for a moment. The waitress placed his second sandwich in front of him, gave him a flirtatious glace, and made her way back to the counter.

'True, I like Roberto,' he said. 'But I like you too… and, as it's that bastard, Mad Dog…'

'So you know where they are?'

'Of course! He keeps them in a box in his garage.' Pascal's eyes danced with mischief. 'Okay, I can find you the tape. I don't know exactly when I will next go to Roberto's place, but I can get it. This time next week, I think. Okay?'

'Really?'

'It will be my pleasure. Together, we will catch the dog. It will be our secret? Yes?' Pascal took another monster bite of his sandwich. 'One condition.'

'Anything.'

'You get lunch,' he said with a smirk.

'I was going to, anyway.'

'I must leave you now,' he announced dramatically, standing up, taking the remnants of his lunch with him.

He looked deep into Rosie's eyes, and held onto her hand a little longer than necessary.

'Rosie, my dear…' His voice was low and husky. It felt to Rosie like everyone in the room, male and female, was watching.

'Out with it then, you big flirt,' Rosie said, smiling. Pascal really had the knack of making a woman feel special.

'I will do it… I will do it for you,' he whispered, before kissing her on both cheeks, and disappearing out of the food hall.

six

The call to Mr Slick-and-Slimy was never going to be an easy one to make. Eddie's business – some sort of import/export enterprise – was based in a vast office overlooking the river. He surrounded himself there with all things garish and crass... right down to the young woman who answered Rosie's call.

'Mullins Exports, Sharon speaking. 'Ow can I 'elp.'

Rosie didn't recognise her voice. Sharon was obviously new. 'Can I speak to Eddie?'

'You mean Mr Mullins. Who can I say is calling? And what is it regarding?'

'Could you tell him it's Rosie.'

'Rosie *who*? What is it in connection with?' Rosie detected a slight hint of jealousy in young Sharon's voice. Perhaps Mr Mullins was more than just a boss to her.

'Just tell him it's Rosie Mullins,' Rosie said abruptly.

Young Sharon's voice and attitude suddenly changed. 'Sorry, Mrs Mullins. Putting you through.'

Now comes the difficult bit, thought Rosie.

'Rosie,' came the crowing voice, which made her instinctively cringe. 'Long time, no hear. How are you? Still as gorgeous as ever? I spoke to Johnny the other day, you know. Interesting conversation, that'

'Forget the niceties. I need to see you.'

After a brief pause, came the reply: 'Oh, right. If it's about Johnny, I've got nothing to say to you. If you haven't got –'

'No!' Rosie snapped, stopping him dead in his tracks. 'It's not about Johnny. It's about you. Meet me at Southend Pier at noon tomorrow.'

'You what?' Eddie stuttered, clearly taken aback. 'Who you fucking talking to?'

'Just be there, Eddie. Believe me, it's in your best interest.'

'It better fucking be,' Eddie growled.

Before he could say anything else, Rosie hung up.

The call must have intrigued Eddie, because even though Rosie was 20 minutes early, he was already waiting for her. She could hardly miss the huge monster of a man standing, feet plonked wide apart, at the entrance.

Southend Pier is all right on a warm sunny day but when there's a north-easterly wind blowing, it's not the place to be. Rosie was pleased that she was wearing her new coat – the one Stevie had given her – to keep her warm, but the bracing wind was making her cheeks tingle. There was only one other person on the pier – a slightly portly, middle-aged man, who was looking over the waves and smoking a cigarette. *A friend of Eddie's?*

She was prepared for a barrage of cruel insults from Eddie, but his attitude completely knocked her off guard. He was playing the smiling viper, not the growling gorilla that she had expected.

'You're looking great, love,' he said, kissing her on the cheek.

The sea was churning white foam, crashing against the pillars beneath them as they walked to the café at the end of the pier. The place was deserted and, as Rosie chose a table, Eddie fetched them a pot of stewed tea from the Formica-topped counter.

'That's better,' he said, with a smile. Smiles always looked wrong on Eddie's face.

Rosie watched Eddie as he arranged the china cups. His fingers, fat like sausages, struggled to fit into the dainty handles, so instead he pinched them between his thumb and forefinger.

'Shall I be mother?'

Rosie didn't flinch, she just looked him in the eyes and said, 'Cut the bullshit, Eddie.'

'Okay,' he sneered, 'have it your way. What the fuck do you want?'

Rosie knew that this confrontation had the potential to blow up in her face. Her life depended on the outcome, so she knew she had to sound confident, calm and precise. Drawing on all of her years of acting, she began to bargain.

'I want out,' she said. 'I want the money you are supposed to give me every month, *and* I want it backdated. I want what is due to me, and due to your niece, Ruby.'

Eddie stared straight back, expressionless. Rosie took a breath and continued, her heart felt like it could give at any moment, 'You started messing me about with the money over four years ago, Eddie – filling me with empty promises. And ever since then I've struggled. I'm behind with the mortgage, with Ruby's school fees. You know I've left Johnny, obviously. Now, I want a divorce. I want the phone calls to stop, and I want you to call off whoever it is that Johnny has set on me.'

There was a moment of uneasy silence as Eddie finished pouring the tea. Finally, he looked up. His eyed were pitch black, like they were swallowing the light.

'You,' he said, slowly and deliberately, but with unmistakable rage, 'ain't getting fuck all, you little slag. You're Rosie Mullins, and you will always be Rosie Mullins. You will *never* mug Johnny off.' Eddie spooned two sugars into his cup before continuing. 'You try to leave and I will slit your pretty, little throat. Do I make myself clear?'

Rosie's heart stopped dead for a second before regaining its frantic rhythm. Her hands were shaking as she unzipped her bag and reached inside. Taking out the videotape, she placed it on the grubby table among the condiments and spilt sugar. She put a finger onto it and, slowly, guided it over towards Eddie.

'What's this?' he said.

'Watch this on your own,' she replied, in no more than

a whisper. 'I have copies. If I don't get what I've asked for or you try and find out how I got it, I'll send your wife a copy, I'll send your children's school a copy, and I'll send your hoity-toity golf buddies a copy.'

Eddie was unsettled. She hadn't seen him like this since Johnny's trial. 'Let me get this right – are you blackmailing me, Rosie Mullins?'

'I *am* a Mullins. You remember that,' she said, leaning forward. 'I suppose that everything I've seen and heard over the years must have rubbed off on me.'

Rosie got up, her legs threatening to give way beneath her.

'Watch the tape, Eddie. Then ring me. I want the money I'm owed. I want to be left alone. And I want to get on with my life, minus the Mullins clan.' She took a few steps to the door, before turning and adding, 'If anything happens, anything at all, to me or my family, I swear to God, Eddie, the copies are all ready to be sent. I'll speak to you later.'

As Rosie walked back along the windy pier, she fought to catch her breath. With every step she took, her confidence grew. She'd done it!

That, she said to herself, *was an Oscar-winning performance.*

Later that evening Rosie received the call. It was short, but very sweet. By the end of the week, a brown manila envelope containing ten grand had been pushed through her letterbox.

Her bank balance was back in the black for the first

time in ages, Ruby's school fees were paid, on time, and there were no unwelcome phone calls. She even called Roberto at the club and told him she was leaving, to focus on her acting again.

'Oh my God!' cried Stevie, who was by now back in the States. 'That's fantastic news! I wish I'd been there when you had that big oaf by the short and curlies. I *told* you it would work!'

seven

About a week after the money arrived, Rosie had taken Annie, her agent, out for dinner. She told her that she was, at last, available to take any audition that was going. Much to Rosie's relief, it wasn't long before she was making the trek to and from Soho to be seen for a variety of roles – commercials, mostly, but a few more exciting parts, too.

One Thursday morning, just after she had come in from hanging the washing on the line, the phone rang. Rosie was tempted to let it ring – over the last week she had had three calls from Johnny. They had not been threatening in nature, but they had still disturbed her. He had begged her to come and visit – 'I want you,' he'd pleaded. 'I *need* you, to survive.' It was clear that he just couldn't accept that it was over.

So it was with some trepidation that Rosie picked up the receiver.

'Hello?'

'Hi, Rosie,' chirped the female voice enthusiastically.

'Oh, morning Annie.'

'Well, congratulations, my dear,'

Rosie held her breath... there was one particularly exciting job she'd been up for, and she was praying to every saint in the calendar that Annie was calling about that one.

'A lead role in a major TV adaptation... that's a bit more than you were expecting, eh?'

The shock sent a giant bolt through her body. 'You mean ... no... it can't be!'

'That's right,' said Annie, after an involuntary tut, 'Eliza Dolittle, *My Fair Lady*! Do you think you could pass as a cockney flower girl who pretends to be a lady?'

'Oh my *God*!' Rosie squealed. She had been really nervous at the audition and didn't think that it had gone particularly well. Let's face it, she was no Audrey Hepburn. But Andrew Brook-Fields, the producer, had been there, and seeing an even *slightly* familiar face had helped to put her at ease. Rosie had been mortified when she had let him down before, so she had been desperate to impress him this time.

'Eliza Dolittle' she grinned.

'Eliza bloody Dolittle!'

'All I want is a room some where,' Rosie began to sing, in her broadest cockney accent, 'far away from the cold night air '

'Wouldn't it be luv-er-ly?' Annie sang, joining in. 'I'll know more about the details later. We'll have a script by the weekend – it's been adapted from the stage version –

and I believe Andrew Brook-Fields is going to contact you personally. I passed on your number.'

'Ain't it bloody luverly?' Rosie exclaimed again, before they said their goodbyes.

Rosie's head was buzzing. She jumped onto the sofa, threw the cushions into the air, and started singing – Rosie was so happy, she couldn't contain it. This was beyond anything she had hoped for.

She couldn't wait to tell somebody... anybody. Her hands still shaking with excitement, she punched in Ruby's phone number. She must be in class, thought Rosie, as the call was directed to her voicemail. Next she tried Aunt Madge – but there was no answer there either... she must be out walking Dibble. *OK... Stevie...*

'Hello?' said the mumbling voice at the end of the line. In her excitement, Rosie had forgotten that it must be something like 4 o'clock in the morning in Florida.

'No *way!*' exclaimed Stevie, after Rosie told her the news. 'Eliza Dolittle! Sweetie, I'm *so* pleased for you. Bless your heart! Oh my God.... Oh my God, Eliza *Dolittle*! I can't wait to tell Joe.'

'I can hear,' came Joe's sleepy voice, as he leaned over to share the phone's mouthpiece with Stevie. 'Congratulation, Rosie. That's great news. I would be even more excited if you'd told me at breakfast.'

'Ignore the grumpy man,' Stevie said.

'Sorry, Joe!' Rosie shouted into the phone, laughing.

'I bet Ruby-two-shoes is thrilled to mint balls!'

When Ruby finally arrived back from school – which seemed to take forever – she dropped her school bag at the foot of the stairs, unwound her scarf… and stopped dead. She hadn't seen her mum this excited or happy, ever.

'What?' she asked, with a puzzled look on her little face.

'I've got it, Ruby darling! I've got it!'

'What, Mum? You got what?'

'That lead role that I auditioned for. Eliza Dolittle!'

Ruby was ecstatic. Not only was she happy for Rosie, but also secretly chuffed at the prospect of living with an actual celebrity.

'My famous mum!' she beamed, throwing her arms out.

The script arrived early on Saturday morning by motorbike courier. Ruby excitedly signed the docket, and took the padded envelope from the rider.

'Mum, Mum it's here!'

Rosie made them a cup of tea, and they cuddled up on the tatty sofa. Rosie began to read.

'"Act One",' she declaimed. '"On a rainy night in Edwardian London the opera patrons were waiting under the arches of Covent Garden for Hackney cabs. Eliza Dolittle, a cockney flower girl, runs into a young man…"'

They were 20 pages in before Ruby noticed a sheet of paper that was still in the envelope.

'Wow, Mum' Ruby said, her eyes like saucers. 'Have you seen this?'

Rosie picked Ruby up, dropped her into her lap, and read the cast list over her shoulder.

'"Eliza Dolittle – Rosie Mullins."' Ruby clapped excitedly. '"Henry Higgins –
Thomas R Williams. Colonel Hugh Pickering – Sir Laurence James." Mum! Simon R James! He's *wicked*. He's been in *everything*. And Sir Laurence James! Flippin' heck!'

Ruby bounced about on the sofa, overwhelmed that her own mum had been cast alongside some of Britain's finest actors.

'Mum?'

'What'

'Oh my *gosh*, I am *so* proud of you.'

eight

On the morning of Rosie's last visit, Johnny had woken earlier than normal. The hands on the clock crawled towards the hour of Rosie's arrival until, at long last, he was summoned.

The bulging veins in his neck pulsed as he strolled along the landing on Cell Block B, mumbling to himself. This short walk to the visiting hall always stirred up strong emotions. This time he had an uneasy feeling, gnawing away in the pit of his stomach, that something was wrong. And not without reason – Rosie hadn't written in over two weeks. That had never happened before. He had to see her, look her in the eye, and find out what the hell was happening.

Like anyone who has spent time inside, his whole world revolved around his visits. After all, there was very little else for him to think about, to occupy his mind. Everything was regimented; he didn't even have to think about where the next meal was coming from. He couldn't go anywhere – there's no bus or train for him to catch. So it was no surprise that the main event of the month was the precious, two-hour visit. Of course, the worst thing that a visitor can do is be late.

For the first few years Rosie had been a dutiful prison wife, making the long journey to go and visit him as regular as clockwork. But, as time passed, with Ruby being so young and having to go round to Aunt Madge's house, she was frequently delayed. That used to wind Johnny up worse than anything. *Didn't she understand that every second he spent with her was gold?* She used every excuse under the sun: 'There was a lot of traffic on the road', 'My train was late'… *blah, blah, blah.* They only had *two* hours – two hours a *month.* Johnny didn't want to miss a second, let alone half an hour. And what made it worse was, when she was late, it usually meant another 30 minutes of him being forced to listen to Rosie's tearful excuses. The cracks in their marriage were there long before he went inside, he knew that, but he wasn't willing to discuss it in their brief time together. Instead, he just got angry.

From the moment that the jury delivered that 'guilty' verdict, Johnny had been afraid that he was going to lose Rosie. He realised that, with him serving an 18-year sentence and their marriage already in trouble, it would only be a matter of time before he got the big heave-ho, the elbow, the goona. Whatever you call it, Johnny knew it was coming.

Each time she was late, his paranoia would kick in and he would start thinking that she wasn't going to turn up at all. Sure, they'd had their fights before he went inside… but that was when the coke really had a grip on him. Even though he was inside, drugs were easily available. He was still using, occasionally, but they didn't have the hold on him that they used to. He was clear-headed enough to know that, in his heart, he didn't want to lose Rosie. He tried to think logically about what to do, and reason it through. But prison doesn't teach you how to be logical, just paranoid.

In retrospect, during those first years away, Johnny had lived his life through Rosie, expecting her to do all the things he wasn't able to. He hadn't thought about her life – being alone in the outside world, with little Ruby. He assumed that Eddie was providing financially, but how she was feeling – mentally, physically, emotionally – that was anyone's guess.

And it wasn't just the monthly visits – Johnny demanded that she wrote twice a week. In Maidstone prison mail was distributed every Tuesday and Friday. Regular as clockwork, Johnny would start to get anxious the night before letter day. He would pace around his cell until the early hours, only ever pausing to wipe the sweat from his palms onto the front of his trousers, and worrying that the next letter would be a 'Dear John'.

No sooner had the officers unlocked his cell, he would holler: 'Where's my letter, where's my letter?'

If there was one, he would retreat to his cell, sit on his

bed, and stare at the envelope, hoping and praying that it contained a 'love you and miss you' note, and not the dreaded alternative.

And if he didn't get one, he would make the officers go through the bundles, checking and double checking. Eventually he would give up, storm back into his cell, and kick the wall. It was on those days that Johnny was best left well alone.

One person who made the mistake of not avoiding Johnny one letter-less Friday was his old mate Transit Nick, who had recently arrived at Maidstone on a six-month lay down.

'Transit Nick' was so named because he used to live in a van, not, as the police thought, because he had been a drug courier. Transit Nick had been a mate of Johnny's for years, and they had worked together on numerous occasions... armed robberies, mostly. Johnny and Transit Nick had served time together elsewhere, and Johnny, although he was loath to admit it, used to consider him a close friend. After all, in the past they had always looked out for each other. But their relationship had never been an easy one. The only thing that Transit Nick loved more than getting into a fight himself, was to see Johnny fight; he loaded the gun, and Johnny would fire it.

Soon after Johnny was moved to Maidstone, he had heard through the grapevine that Transit Nick had turned bad, that he was 'a wrong 'un'. This was not only dangerous, but also a real kick in the teeth for Johnny, who had considered him a friend. At first, he couldn't believe it. *How could I have got him so wrong?* It really knocked him back that he was a no-good grass. And in Johnny's world, there was no room for a grass. To make matters worse, the word was that Transit Nick had grassed on an old mate that Johnny and Eddie used to go out on jobs with. Yes, Transit Nick had turned out to be a right old mongrel.

So when Transit Nick arrived at Maidstone prison, Johnny decided that his number was up. *He's played his games for long enough.* Johnny was going to hurt him, and hurt him bad, so that when Transit Nick looked in the mirror every morning, he'd see something to remember him by.

If you're inside and want to hurt someone, you need a blade, which were pretty hard to come by, or a piece of glass. Glass is a rare commodity, and the only available substitute was in the form of Johnny's hair-cream jar. Johnny waited, patiently watching, day by day, as the hair cream slowly ran down. In prison, Johnny had learnt to be a fairly patient man, which was something that didn't come naturally to him.

He had intended to wait until he had used up the last of the hair cream, but one Friday he had seen Transit Nick talking to a screw. And not just a quick, 'hello, goodbye', but a real conversation. For Johnny, it was like Transit Nick advertising that he was a no-good grass. So Johnny rushed to his cell, smashed the bottle of hair cream, and, with cold precision, sharpened one edge on the stone windowsill. By the time that Johnny's wing was called to the exercise yard, it was as sharp as a razor. He carefully wrapped a thin strip of old shirt material around the bottom half of the makeshift knife, slipped it into the pocket of his donkey jacket, and strolled out into the yard.

It didn't take long to spot Transit Nick, and when he did, he couldn't take his eyes off him. Transit Nick was laughing and chatting with another prison officer, clearly oblivious to the danger that he was facing. When Johnny did, eventually, look around the yard, he was given a sharp reminder that this was not the best venue for what he had planned. There was plenty of activity, lots of ears and eyes. Johnny quickly called over two cons, who he knew were prepared to do whatever was asked of them. He arranged a distraction – a mock fight on the opposite side of the exercise yard.

As Johnny lit a cigarette, a whistle blew, signalling the end of the recreation period. Johnny quickly got into line behind Transit Nick, knelt down, and re-tied the lace on his right shoe. On seeing the signal, a wailing voice came from the other end of the yard. '*What* did you fucking say?' Within seconds, the two cons were at each others throats and, on cue, the screws quickly ran over to break up the fight.

Johnny took a last drag, and dropped the cigarette to the dusty ground, grinding it out with the heel of his shoe. Quick as a flash, he grabbed Transit Nick by the hair, forcing his head back, and whipped the glass knife across his throat. It was over in a matter of seconds.

Everyone around Nick withdrew, in an almost perfect circle, as he fell to his knees, his hands desperately grasping

69

at his throat, as if his fingers could repair the damage. He tried to scream, but there were no words, just a garbled, bloody mumbling. His eyes bulged as the blood poured relentlessly from his veins. He looked around at the inmates surrounding him, his face contorted with fear and panic, before collapsing. By the time the screws had clocked that something serious had happened, and run back, Transit Nick was twitching on the bloody, damp ground. All the cons were already wearing their familiar 'I didn't see nothing' expressions. They knew better than to grass on Johnny Mullins.

Within minutes, with the alarm blaring and whistles blowing, Transit Nick was carted off to the hospital. Johnny didn't give a fuck if he had killed him or not.

Johnny's head was a tangled mess of emotions and memories that morning of the visit. He had been gearing up for seeing Rosie, and wanted things to be *right*… he wanted it so much it hurt. He had woken up in a good mood, and had even caught himself humming as he washed and shaved. He splashed on a generous amount of Davidoff Cool Water, his favourite cologne, and turned to the photograph of Rosie hanging next to his bunk. He wanted to look his best.

He'd been thinking about what he was going to say to her all night. He just wanted to put things right between them, even if that meant swallowing his pride and apologising to her… after all, it doesn't matter who says sorry as long as someone does. And today, he decided that he was going to be the one to do it. Every time he thought of Rosie his belly flipped over, and a warm feeling of anticipation swept over him.

When he first saw it, the visitor's area in Maidstone Prison reminded Johnny of a school's assembly hall... albeit one with five prison officers sitting behind a blue guard rail on the stage at the far end. At the other end of the hall is the control unit, manned by a solitary officer but guarded by eight others. Across the ceiling, along the blue, wrought-iron girders, the dome-like security cameras rotate periodically, winking their red lights, monitoring every move. There are about 40 tables, all numbered, each one surrounded by four chairs – three beige and one brown – all screwed to the floor.

When Johnny arrived in the hall and saw Rosie waiting there, his heart was pounding. Johnny looked her up and down as he made his way over to where she was sitting. She looked gorgeous, absolutely stunning. *Although that blouse is a bit low cut... and that make-up is a bit over the top.* Glancing around, he saw that he wasn't the only one admiring her. *And is that that red nail varnish?* It was. That tarty red nail varnish, which she *knew* he didn't like. If he'd told her once, he'd told her a thousand times: only tarts wear red nail varnish.

Once he had sat down, instead of saying what he wanted to say – how pleased he was to see her, how beautiful she looked – he started talking about her nails. The words came tumbling out. Almost immediately, Johnny wished he could take them back, but it was too late – Rosie was already in tears. He tried to pacify her, calm her down, but as he put his arm around her she angrily pulled away.

'Johnny, look… I have something I have to tell you.'

'What,' Johnny asked, instinctively. But he already knew. There had been no letters for over a fortnight, and now she had to *something to tell him.*

Johnny could hardly remember the walk from the visiting hall to his cell. He was consumed and disorientated by disappointment… and anger. Angry with the screws, angry with the other cons, angry with the fucking walls that kept him pent up, angry with Rosie, and, perhaps most of all, angry with himself. He felt worthless. He loved Rosie, but it seemed that all he could do was push her away. Not that he ever really admitted that to himself – his male pride and arrogance wouldn't allow him to be wrong. Johnny coped in the only way he knew how: blaming everybody but himself, and lashing out.

Once the initial shock and anger had burnt away, Johnny filled his days with thinking about what he could do or say to get Rosie back. Searing embers of resentment still glowed inside and his temper would flare up every time he called and got the answering machine. He was tearing through every phone card he could get his hands on, but when Rosie did actually pick up, her answer was always the same:

'I don't want it any more Johnny, I want to be respectable – I just want out.'

nine

R osie was reading the contract that had been hand-
delivered, completely engrossed in the figures
swimming in front of her.

'I'm going to Auntie Madge's. We're taking Dibble for
a walk. Are you coming?'

Silence.

'Mum! Do you wanna come and take Dibble for a *walk?*'

'Sorry Rube…what was that?' Rosie mumbled, still not
taking much notice. She just couldn't believe it. Was
someone seriously going to pay her that much, for
something she would willingly do for nothing? Annie had
certainly earned her 17.5%, by the looks of things.

Trying to draw her mum's attention Ruby asked: 'I
don't think you enjoy taking Dibble for walks, do you?
Not really your thing.'

'Nah, you're probably right,' Rosie said, turning the
page. She kept checking that it was, in fact, *her* name at the
top of the contract.

'Well, I'd better go. Aunt Madge will be waiting for me.'

'Okay, you have a lovely time, the two of you,' said Rosie, still not looking up, before adding, 'I'll get a pizza for tea.'

'Don't you ever listen to *anything* I say?' said Ruby, carrying her school bag into the kitchen. 'I told you, I'm staying at Auntie Madge's. She's made a shepherd's pie. We're watching *Strictly* and *X-Factor*.'

'Sorry darling,' said Rosie, sliding the contract off the table and onto a chair, 'Mummy wasn't listening.'

Just then, the phone started to ring. Ruby moved towards the door.

'Don't I get a kiss?' Rosie called after her.

Spinning on her heels, Ruby returned and planted a peck on her cheek. Before she could zoom off again, Rosie had grabbed her in a giant bear hug.

'Okay, off you go' she said, turning to the phone.

Not needing any encouragement, Ruby grabbed her bag and ran out, slamming the door behind her.

Rosie reached for the phone.

'Hello?'

'Rosie, it's Andrew Brook-Fields.'

Rosie felt her heart leap, partly because she had expected it to be Auntie Madge calling to see where Ruby had got to, but mostly because Andrew's voice had such a smooth, rich and sophisticated tone that it was impossible to resist.

Casting a quick glance out of the front door and seeing that Ruby had already skipped up the road, she felt free to inject equal warmth into her own voice.

'Hi, how are you, Andrew?'

'I'm fine, I hope it's okay to call you... out of the blue. I wanted to catch you before your schedule got too full to squeeze in a lunch. Tuesday or Thursday any good?'

'That will be lovely,' said Rosie. 'I think it may have to be Tuesday, because I'm pencilled in for a costume fitting on the Thursday.'

'Then Tuesday it is. I'll be at my office in the morning, in Soho... but if it's not convenient to come into town, I'd be happy to –'

'I'm meeting the publicist in Covent Garden at three-thirty, so that should work out well,' she interjected.

'Ah! Well, that's very good timing, then. I was hoping to have a chat with you before they got their hands on you. So shall we say one o'clock at Joe Allen's? I'll text you my mobile number, just in case anything crops up. So... I'll see you then.'

'Yes, see you Tuesday.'

'By the way, congratulations. We're thrilled to have you on board.'

'Thank you' she said softly. 'I'm thrilled too.'

Rosie found it so energizing to be in the heart of the West End again, and it showed – she had a wide, beaming smile stretching from ear to ear. She felt alive and carefree as she strolled confidently through the bustling, cluttered streets of Soho. Everything, from the noise of the traffic to the vibrant mix of people rushing around, was like an electric charge shooting straight through her veins. At long last she didn't feel like some dolly bird who only turned heads because of her long legs. She was a creditable, recognised actress – or, at least, she would be very soon.

Rosie wasn't even nervous about her lunch meeting. On any other day, even the thought of going to see Andrew Brook-Fields would have made her quake. He was, after all, a real big cheese, known to virtually everyone who worked in the media. Thanks to a string of successful dramas, made by Straw/Gold Productions – his own company, with offices in London and Bristol – his name was one of the most highly respected in the business. Knowing that Andrew trusted Rosie with such an important role in his next project was so exhilarating that she couldn't help but feel good.

Joe Allen's is a fashionable restaurant just off Covent Garden, in the heart of theatre land. Rosie found the discreet entrance and looked at her watch – three minutes early. After straightening her clothes she made her way down the cool stairway to the trendy basement, with its exposed brickwork, plastered with show posters, photos, and programmes. She was greeted by the Maître d'.

'Good Afternoon,' he said. 'Table for…?'

'No, actually. I'm joining someone,' Rosie replied, as she handed the cloakroom assistant her coat. 'I'm not sure if they're here yet.'

'Ah, I see. What name is the booking under? '

Swelling with pride, Rosie replied, 'Andrew Brook-Fields.'

'Mr Brook-Fields is already at his table,' the maître d' announced.

The restaurant was buzzing. A delicious, pungent smell of roasted garlic hung in the air, mingling with a burble of mostly male voices. Rosie followed the maître d', negotiating her way along a path littered with briefcases and laptops. They passed the long bar, which was crowded with journalists, actors, and smartly dressed businessmen with their associates on extended business lunches, sipping Bloody Marys in the soft, hazy lighting. As they approached the table, Andrew Brook-Fields put the menu down and rose to his feet. Rosie's cheeks flushed pink as her eyes locked with his – they were penetrating, ridiculously brown, and probing her every move.

'Hi!' he said, leaning forward and kissing Rosie on both cheeks.

'Hi.'

'I think you have just made me the envy of every man in the room!'

Rosie suspected that, in fact, the opposite was true. Walking towards the table, she noticed that a female diner was occasionally glancing over at Andrew. Not that she could blame her – Andrew Brook-Fields was certainly handsome, with his greying, almost silver, hair. He was well dressed, too; his brown silk shirt was a perfect match to complement his eyes. Rosie wondered if that was a coincidence. *Probably not.*

Andrew pulled out Rosie's chair, flashing her a smile as she sat down. When he smiled, his white teeth looked even more dazzling against his tan, which was so rich that he could almost pass as Mediterranean. He had an unmistakable air of confidence about him, which immediately made Rosie feel relaxed and safe. Being as successful as he was, Rosie thought, he had nothing to prove and, so, no need to waste his time caring about trends or images, or what anybody else might think.

After they had settled in their seats, the maître d' went to seat a middle-aged man who had entered the restaurant shortly after Rosie. Andrew shot her a mischievous look.

'Why don't we start with a glass of champagne, to toast your success?' he suggested. 'Unless, perhaps, you'd rather keep a clear head for your meeting?'

'I doubt one glass will do much harm,' she replied, coyly. 'Besides, I suspect that I have you to thank for my turn in fortunes.'

After signalling the waiter, Andrew ordered two glasses of the best champagne on the wine list.

'So, how surprised were you to get Eliza Dolittle?'

'On a scale of one to ten...' said Rosie, her eyes widening, 'I think it would zoom off into space. Honestly, I had no idea I was being considered for the lead when I auditioned.' Her eyes narrowed playfully. 'Did you?'

Seeming almost pleased by the challenge, Andrew said, 'Not initially, but when I saw the tapes from your first audition, it occurred to me that we should, at least, bear you in mind.' Andrew took a sip of champagne before continuing. 'After watching the screen test, the decision was unanimous. As I'm sure you know, beautiful women don't always photograph well. You're a real find.'

Feeling slightly embarrassed, Rosie dropped her eyes to

Andrew's hands resting on the table. They were beautifully manicured. Realising their elegant masculinity was having an effect on her, she looked up at him again.

'I shall do my very best, Andrew. I won't let you down.'

'I know.'

'This is a dream role for me. I'll give it one hundred percent.' She looked him directly in the eyes, and smiled. 'Thank you to *everyone* at Straw/Gold. And to you in particular. This is a great opportunity.'

As they touched glasses, Andrew's eyes lingered on Rosie, and a subtle, but unmistakeably pleasurable sensation, swelled inside her.

'So, tell me about you,' Andrew asked, after a loaded pause. 'Married? Kids?'

'Well, yes,' she said, quickly adding 'but we're not together any more.' Rosie took another sip of champagne. 'I have a daughter. Her name's Ruby. Twelve, going on eighteen.'

'Really? I know the type.'

Rosie nodded. 'Do you have any children?'

'Yes,' he relied, nodding slowly. 'I have an ex-wife, and two step-daughters. My ex lives in Berkshire now with her new partner and the girls.'

Just then the menus arrived. By the time they had decided what to eat, the subject had returned to the business.

'Ordinarily,' said Andrew, 'the director will be taking you to lunch. But as Stella is one of the topics I want to discuss, I thought it should just be you and me. Anyway, you'll meet her properly at that lunch next week…

the one the executive producer and production manager are hosting.'

'So what about Stella?'

'Well,' said Andrew, clearly choosing his words carefully. 'However stern, authoritarian or uncompromising she might seem, Stella Evans is really a sweetheart. I just wanted to tell you that, for goodness sake, don't make the mistake of taking anything personally. You'll have her full support, and you will soon discover that she is a first-rate director. But – and it's a big 'but' – she doesn't see her work as a popularity contest. She just wants to make excellent dramas, which is something she has an excellent track record of doing. Believe me, she could win awards for this one.'

'She sounds scary,' said Rosie. 'She won't bite me, will she?'

'No!' laughed Andrew. His laugh made her laugh too.

'I'll admit, I've heard how scary she can be. I was a little nervous… now I think I'm terrified!'

'I don't think you'll have too much trouble standing up to her,' said Andrew, still laughing. 'And please do so. She has a lot of time for gutsy characters. In fact, your genuine, East End persona was a major factor in you getting the job. We could have chosen someone more accomplished, but you can't *learn* that true, street grit. You're born with it. We wanted to inject some realism in the story… and you fitted the bill perfectly.'

Sitting back in her chair, almost to physically escape the pull of his charm, Rosie said, 'So how involved will you be in the shoot?'

'On a day-to-day basis, not very,' he replied. 'I will probably be on-set once or twice a month, depending on commitments. I'll be more hands-on in the post-production, and keep an eye on the editing. I might give a few pointers, but only ever through Stella Evans, never directly. She's a safe pair of hands.'

The waiter returned with their food, and Rosie watched as the Waldorf salad she had ordered was set down in front of her. In spite of how delicious it looked, she knew she was far too excited to manage more than a couple of mouthfuls.

'The next subject I wanted to cover,' Andrew continued, as the waiter reappeared with an enormous pepper mill, 'is publicity. You were in *EastEnders*, so you'll have a vague idea already of how much is going to come your way. Obviously, once it's broadcast, public interest – and more to the point, media interest – will really intensify. My advice to you is to make a friend of the press. Be available, up to a point that's reasonable. Be charming and accommodating, again within reason. But whatever you do, don't lie to them. They're a foxy lot and, if you do, they'll find out. The last thing you want is for them to turn against you.'

He took a mouthful of food and poured them both some water.

'I know what I'm saying is basic common sense,' he went on, 'and the publicist will go over it again this afternoon. I'm just keen to stress how important it is for you to start dealing with any skeletons that you might have in your cupboard now. A stitch in time saves nine, so to speak. Presuming you have some skeletons – and, let's face it, most of us do – you could do yourself an enormous favour by outing them now, right at the beginning. That way, you should have nothing to fear from some slimy young hack who's trying to get "the scoop of the year".

'Believe me, Rosie, once you step foot into the public arena, you open yourself and your family up to media scrutiny. Everything's considered fair game.'

'I see,' said Rosie, deep in thought.

'This is the point at which I invite you to tell me your deepest, darkest secrets,' said Andrew, with a twinkle in his eye. 'It's okay, you don't have to answer. This is simply to get you to think about what I am saying, so you can assess the situation, before you start spilling the beans.'

'There is one thing, Andrew, that I ought to mention,' Rosie heard herself say.

'Yes?' Andrew tilted his head to one side, appearing neither shocked nor worried, just mildly intrigued.

'It's Ruby's father. He's in prison.'

'Mmm, I see. Do you mind me asking what the offence was?'

'Drugs,' said Rosie, reluctantly. She knew that a drugs conviction has a certain stigma attached to it, and saying the word made her cringe.

'What sort of drug offence? Are we talking serious? Misdemeanour?'

Rosie hunched her shoulders and shrunk back into her

seat. This was excruciating, she wanted the ground to open up and swallow her.

'Serious, I'm afraid. Well, serious enough for him to be sentenced to eighteen years.'

'Eighteen years!' exclaimed Andrew, sitting bolt upright. 'Goodness me!'

Almost too afraid to say the words, Rosie said, in a hushed whisper, 'Yes, eighteen years, for drug importation.'

'I see. Well, I'm sorry to say that this is *exactly* the sort of thing I was talking about. You should get it out right from the start. Tell the story your way, before someone jumps on the bandwagon and uses it for their own gain.'

'Which is inevitable,' she muttered, looking down at her barely touched plate of food.

'I'm afraid it is.'

Suddenly, and violently, Rosie was hit by another thought. It flashed into her head with such dizzying speed that her heartbeat actually halted. *The other secret...* the one she had only ever confided in Stevie. Once her face was out there, someone would be sure to recognise her.

'Until recently...' she said, then paused. *This could ruin everything.* She took a deep, unsteady breath. 'Until recently, I was working at a gentlemen's club called the Keyhole, in Mayfair.'

Immediately her cheeks started to burn, certain that the connotations must already be obvious. 'My job primarily was behind the scenes, in the offices. But occasionally – well, twice to be precise – I worked in the club as a hostess... greeting clients, taking their coats, showing them to the private rooms.' Though Andrew's eyes were firmly fixed on his food, she could tell he was listening intently.

'The kind of things...' she stopped and started again. 'The financial situation had become... Ruby needed...'

She took a sip of water before trying again. 'I'm not sure if you know what this means, Andrew?' She paused, hoping she wouldn't have to spell it out.

'I think so.' He nodded. 'But it can depend on the kind of place we are talking about. What sort of club is the Keyhole, Rosie?'

'Well... the Keyhole is a little more... how can I put this? Up market than some, I think. Like all the hostesses, I worked... you know... without much on. I can't speak for what everyone gets up to in the private rooms. I only know what happened on those two nights.'

'Mmm.' Andrew nodded soberly. Rosie suddenly felt so ashamed, and wondered if mentioning it was a big mistake. After all, it might never have got out.

'I didn't do anything,' she said, hastily. 'Honestly, I didn't. I had offers, but I refused. And if anyone ever says any different, they'd be lying.'

Andrew's eyes came up and met Rosie's. It was obvious how ashamed she looked, as his expression immediately changed.

'You know that I don't judge you in any way for what you did. And that, if this gets out, you would have our *entire* team behind you... lawyers, everyone.' He gave her a reassuring smile. 'And now I am going to say something you probably won't like very much, but here goes anyway

84

– this is exactly the kind of thing that, given the right spin, the publicist will go to town with. You know, they can really turn negatives into positives.

'If you are willing to talk about *why* you worked there – which, by the sounds of it, had a lot to do with providing for your daughter – then the public will support you. Mark my words. You're… sexy, you're glamorous, and it's a mother's sacrifice for her child.'

He was looking straight into Rosie's eyes as he spoke.

'I'm sorry to be so blunt, but I'm sure that's how it's going to read. Men will love you because you look the way you do. Women will empathise, and understand the terrible dilemma that drove you to it – a husband in prison, wife fighting to make ends meet for her daughter… a daughter who has wants and needs, the same as any of their own children. Who wouldn't sacrifice to provide for their child? With the right angle, Rosie, this could work in your favour. And, I'm ashamed to admit, the production's too.'

Rosie swallowed hard and lifted her glass. 'Apart from my best friend, you are the only person I have ever told about this. And you're right, I can see why it would make a good story, but …'

There were so many thoughts rushing around her head that she hardly knew which to tackle first. 'There are other actresses working at the club,' she said finally. 'I know they won't be able to keep it to themselves. So, yes, it would be best if I beat them to it. I'm worried about Ruby, though. And my Aunt Madge, who's more like a mother to me.'

'Then obviously you must tell them before you give the green light to the publicist.'

Rosie nodded. 'Actually,' she went on, 'I'm more concerned about my husband, Johnny. He's… um… I don't know how to put this. Well, he's a gangster. And he is totally unaware that I worked in a gentlemen's club. I think if he read it in a paper or someone told him in prison, he'd be mortified. I'm serious, he'd go ballistic. It would be humiliating for him, the ultimate mug-off. He'd kill me.'

Andrew leaned back into his chair. Rosie could see that he was shocked, but was doing his best to hide it. There was an uncomfortable pause. Rosie looked around at her fellow diners. She briefly made eye contact with the man on the nearby table who had entered soon after her, but he quickly glanced down at his coffee.

'Well, I can't make that decision for you, Rosie, the decision has to be yours,' Andrew said, breaking the silence. 'Secrets don't always come out, you know. If you want to keep it hidden and hope that no one comes forward…'

Rosie shook her head. 'That would be crazy. Even if one of the girls didn't try to sell their story – and I know they will – there are always the men that I encountered. Any of them could easily recognise me. Although, I suppose it's a bit naïve to think anyone was looking at my face.'

That comment finally broke the tension. Andrew stretched back and looked around the restaurant, his eyes lit with humour. He dabbed his mouth with a crisp white napkin.

'Probably,' he said, in a way that made her smile too. 'Look, you get to call the shots. Take some time and think it over. Talk to your family. Then decide whether or not to confide in the publicist. As far as I'm concerned, it will go no further than this table.'

'Thank you,' she said.

An hour or so later, as they stepped out onto the street, taking care to dodge the black Hackney cabs with irate drivers that constantly whizzed up and down, Rosie felt so alive that she could have flung her arms around Andrew and kissed him.

'Okay, so you're off to see the publicist now,' he said, checking his watch. 'And I have a meeting on Goodge Street. Which means we're going in opposite directions. Thanks for coming today, Rosie. I've enjoyed getting to know you a little better.'

'I've enjoyed it too,' she told him, with an enigmatic smile. 'Very much. In fact, having unburdened my sins, I'm so relieved that I'm in danger of gushing. So, let's spare your blushes and make the parting swift.' Rosie held out her hand.

'Consider me gone,' Andrew said, before gently kissing her on both cheeks. 'You have an extremely busy few weeks ahead, but you have my number if you need it. Otherwise, I'll see you at the pre-shoot meeting.'

'I look forward to it,' she said warmly. 'And thanks again.'

'My pleasure.'

ten

'Oh my *God*! That's wicked!' Ruby laughed, her mouth open as wide as the Dartford Tunnel. 'Oh Mum, you really did that?' Then she looked over at Aunt Madge, with her butter-wouldn't-melt-in-her-mouth expression, her grin widening all the time. 'Did you know?'

Aunt Madge shook her head, a little less impressed. 'Not until today.'

Ruby dissolved into giggles. 'You actually took your clothes off, Mum? *All* of them? What on earth were you thinking! I *never* would guess that you'd *ever* do that.' Looking at Aunt Madge again, who was keeping busy, brushing out the tangles in Dibble's coat. 'Why aren't you as surprised as me?'

Aunt Madge tried to play it down. She shrugged, appearing to be more interested in the small dog that was perched on her lap. Of course, Rosie knew that, in reality, she was trying not to make a big issue out it. She was well aware of how she must be feeling after making such an enormous and personal admission.

'Well... I surprised *myself*,' Rosie assured her.

Ruby drew up and dropped her shoulders abruptly, gesturing indifference. 'Who cares?' she said, trying to act all grown up. 'It's so out there! My mother, the major sex symbol. It's so wild!'

Rosie gave her a reassuring smile. Although she was relieved that Ruby was taking it so well, she was reminded how young and naïve her daughter was. Bless her, she really didn't understand the dark, dangerous world that her mother had entered.

Meanwhile, in Maidstone Prison, Johnny sat on the bunk in his cell, staring at the white envelope in his hand. He knew it was from Rosie – he recognised her neat handwriting immediately. He turned the envelope slowly in his hands, over and over again. Considering how their last face-to-face had gone, he honestly hadn't expected any more letters from her.

He scrutinised the envelope as it turned, as if he could somehow divine its contents without opening it. Was it a 'I've made a terrible mistake – I love you' letter? Or the 'I want a divorce' letter? *Let's face it, it's probably the second one.*

Johnny saw that his palms were sweating again, so he wiped them on his trousers before sliding a finger under the flap and tearing open the envelope. Pulling out the white, sweet-smelling paper, he began to read:

Dear Johnny,

I hope you are well. Ruby is fine and doing extremely well at school, she sends her love and a big kiss. I expect you're wondering why I am writing this. Well, I have some good news – no, fantastic news. You know how hard I trained to become an actress, well all that training and hard work has finally paid off. I have been cast in a leading role in a new period drama, playing Eliza Dolittle in My Fair Lady. *I know you have never given my career much thought, but to me it's the big break I have been dreaming about.*

Johnny took a breath and held it. *So far so good.*

I wanted to write and tell you out of respect to you, so you wouldn't hear the news from someone else. As you can imagine, Rube is totally ecstatic at the prospect of having a famous mum.

There is a second reason for me writing to you, Johnny.

Here we go, thought Johnny, *it's the big heave-ho.* With hands that were beginning to shake – with some kind of emotion, but he suspected it was anger – he continued to read...

As you can imagine, I will be getting some coverage on television and in the red tops. For obvious reasons, your name and predicament will be mentioned. Not by me, but by prying journalists trying to dig the dirt. The production company will put a spin on the story and minimise the impact. I have been assured it will be dealt with better if I come clean about the story myself, rather than wait for it to break. You being in prison is something we cannot hide, so we will have to deal with it when it comes. But I promise you that I will not bad mouth you in any way, shape or form.

Johnny shrugged. He didn't care if people knew that he was in prison. Why should he? It was just an occupational hazard and came with the territory.

There's something else that might come out in the papers. Something that you might not like, Johnny, but I have decided be honest with you. I worked a couple of nights at the Keyhole Club in Mayfair. Not doing anything wrong, but in the office doing the books.

Well, I'm signing off now, Johnny. Ruby is running late, and I have to learn my lines. I will write again, and let you know when your famous wife will be on the TV.

Take care, 'bye for now

Rosie and Ruby.

Obviously, Johnny knew exactly what the Keyhole was all about, but he didn't for one minute consider that Rosie would work — as in 'work' — there. But as for shuffling some papers in the office, well, Johnny could accept that. In fact, he wondered why Rosie felt the need to mention it at all.

The most important aspect of the letter was what it *didn't* say: it wasn't the 'Dear John' that he'd be dreading. He re-read it four times, searching for something, anything, that might indicate that Rosie was still in love with him. He tried to convince himself that, because Rosie had written '*your* famous wife', she would be waiting for him on the outside.

His brother Eddie had visited him in prison the week before, to discuss a new 'business venture', and had done his best to persuade Johnny that Rosie was 'just like any bird'.

'Okay, maybe she won't get back with you... but who cares? She's not all that!' he had said. 'But she'll probably come crawling back at some point.'

Women were, Eddie told him, 'funny bloody creatures' who 'change their mind every fucking five minutes'. Johnny had not shared his brother's confidence. Worse still, he couldn't help but feel that Eddie was hiding something from him. The way he talked about Rosie was unusually involved.

'I'm not so sure,' he had said, 'she's seems to have made her mind up all right.'

'Listen to me,' Eddie had told him, 'she's just having one of her little moments. She's probably got the painters and decorators in.' They had both laughed at that one. 'Give the dozy mare a bit of time, she'll be okay. She's Rosie *Mullins* remember?'

'Honestly, I'm up to my eyes with costume fittings, hair

consultations and don't get me started on the publicity. And I've got *so* many lines to learn before the big, pre-shoot meeting on the twenty-first. You should see the size of the script! I need a memory like Rain Man to remember all this.'

Rosie heard Stevie's unmistakable laugh. It was so loud she almost dropped her mobile.

'So,' Stevie asked, 'have there been any shocking revelations in the papers about Rosie Mullins and her disgraceful behaviour?'

'Very funny. No, actually. The press release only went out this morning. But apparently the publicist, Elsie, has already been inundated with interview requests. Well, sex sells, I suppose? I'm due to record a GMTV piece later today.'

'Where are you now?' Stevie asked.

'I'm in the back of a cab, about to be late for a lunch with Stella Evans. Andrew warned me that she's a bit of an ogre.'

'Right,' said Stevie, sarcastically, 'like you're scared of ogres. You're married to one, and you've got an even bigger one for a brother-in-law. Speaking of which, how have they reacted to everything?'

'In actual fact, Johnny has been really cool about it. At least, I think he has. He's left quite a few messages, but none of them were too awful or anything. He even said "Good luck with the film, then",' Rosie said, doing an eerily accurate impersonation of him.

'Well, that's a turn up for the books, isn't it? He's proud of you, I suppose.'

'Pigs might fly! If the truth be known, I think he has other things on his mind. He mentioned that Eddie's been to see him about some deal that they've got going down.'

'Anyway, enough about him. When are you likely to see this Andrew Curly-Wurly again?'

'Brook-Fields.'

'Well, whatever his name is.'

Feeling a pleasurable flip in her tummy, Rosie said, 'Actually, not until the pre-shoot meeting – in a couple of weeks.'

'Well, it sounds like you're keeping busy.'

'It's amazing. Half the time I'm pinching myself to make sure its real, the other half I'm frantic, convinced that it's all about to come crashing down around me.'

'When does filming start?'

'Monday. Honestly, Stevie, part of me is absolutely dreading sitting down and watching it. After all this hype, expectations are going to be so high, I can't see how I can live up to them.'

No sooner had Rosie and Stevie said their goodbyes and hung up, another call came in. Seeing the publicist's name flashing on the display screen of her mobile, Rosie pressed the 'answer' button immediately.

'Hi Elsie!' she said chirpily.

'Hi yourself. Now, you are needed at the Dorchester, to do an interview and photo shoot for the *Mail*.'

'When?' asked Rosie, fumbling in her bag for her diary.

'Sorry to put this on you at such short notice, but how about now? It's just come up. You're already booked in at hotel for a brief shoot at three-thirty, so it works out okay. Tom is going to be joining you for that, and the stylist is on her way. Costume have put some clobber a taxi, which is on its way, and –'

'Hang on, hang on!' Rosie cried. 'I thought I was recording the GMTV interview at five?'

'That's been changed. They're doing it tomorrow morning now, live.'

'Oh my God! Look, before I forget, can you tell Stella? I was meant to meet her for lunch.'

'Already done,' proclaimed Elsie, proudly. 'Where are you now?'

'I'm heading down the Mall, towards Trafalgar Square,' said Rosie, glancing out of the window. Have I got time for lunch?'

'No, no, no. I'll make sure there's something waiting for you at the Dorchester, okay? Got to go now, the phones are going crazy. Call if you need anything.'

Then she was gone. Elsie was a force of nature. Although Rosie had known her for less than a month, she was already, hands down, the most energetic person she had ever come across. With her head spinning, Rosie redirected the cab, and noted the GMTV interview in her diary. As she wrote 'live i/v – GMTV', she already knew she would probably have a sleepless night. It might be stressful, thought Rosie, but this is living.

Considering that they hadn't even started shooting, it was phenomenal how much press she had received. True, she had always wanted to be a success and stand on her own two feet, but, as the cab pulled up outside the grand entrance of the Dorchester, Rosie felt uneasy. She couldn't forget the advice that Aunt Madge had given her all those years ago: *Things that go up quickly usually come down with a huge bump.*

eleven

It was visiting day for Johnny again, and Eddie and Hate-'em-all-Harry were on their way to see him. Hate-'em-all, a big man with large cauliflower ears and a nose as wide as a double wardrobe, was like Eddie's shadow – the brothers' most loyal friend.

Maidstone Prison, one of Britain's oldest jails, is situated right in the very heart of the town. Maidstone itself is well known for its appalling one-way system, with the prison acting as an island, around which the constant stream of traffic is filtered. So, wherever you want to get to in town, you'll pass HMP Maidstone. The traffic whizzes around the nick, with most of the drivers oblivious of the secret world that goes on behind those tall, cold walls. A few of the cells actually overlook the main road, which, for long-term prisoners, makes their sentence even more difficult, as they can personally witness life carrying on outside. And Tuesdays are the worst of all – that's market day in Maidstone. The hustle and bustle of the market penetrates the walls of the imposing, stone fortress, and echoes through the minds of each and every man inside.

Hate-'em-all was chauffeuring Eddie in his pride and joy, a silver Mercedes SL500 with a personalized number plate – EDM1. Throughout the journey from London to Maidstone, Eddie was, as ever, very critical of the way Hate-'em-all was driving. Every time he pushed, pulled and crunched the gears, Eddie would throw him a 'sideways filthy'.

'It's a gearbox, not a fucking jukebox.'

A light rain was falling as they parked and made their way to the huge, medieval-looking oak gates. The journey had not been an easy one, and the reason was that Eddie and Harry loathed visiting anyone in prison, even Johnny. They hated the degrading routine of the endless security checks.

The security was incredibly thorough. First, images of their faces would be electronically transmitted onto a security badge, and their hands placed onto a machine which took an impression. Next, they had to empty their pockets and take off their jackets, which were, in turn, put through an X-ray machine. Then, they would have to go through a metal detector, into a small side-room, where they would be searched from top to toe, including their mouths and under their tongues. Next, it would be back to the corridor, where they would stand still, with their arms by their sides, while a sniffer dog checked for illegal substances. Then on past several more checkpoints, their handprints checked and double checked. Eventually, they would go through a turnstile... like the ones at football matches. A final check of hands, and they would be escorted into the visiting hall and told to sit.

When they finally arrived, Johnny was waiting at table No 12, seated in the inmate's chair, the brown one. He looked fit and well, Eddie thought, dressed in the usual prison uniform of sweatshirt, jeans, and trainers.

Hate-'em-all smiled, noticing the excitement shared by the brothers. The business that they had come to discuss – 'the Panama deal', as they called it – had taken months of meticulous planning.

'I'm all ears,' Johnny said, leaning forward, with a thin smile on his face.

Eddie, especially, was almost beside himself. Conscious of the cameras and the lip-reading skills of the prison guards, he leaned over so he was within an inch of his brother. 'The doors for the extension have arrived!' he said, in a hoarse whisper.

Johnny's eyes widened. 'That was quick... those boys don't muck about.'

'This is the start of something big,' Hate-'em-all said, as the brothers took sips of stewed tea from their Styrofoam cups.

'Yeah. Very big,' said Johnny, greedily unwrapping a Genoa cake and taking a large bite.

Over the course of a few visits, months before, Eddie and Johnny had come up with a sophisticated plan – 'the plan of plans' – involving their contacts in South America.

Eddie had taken a 'holiday' to Panama, posing as a tourist, taking his new secretary, Sharon, with him. He would have preferred, in fact, to have taken one of his boyfriends but, for a trip that sensitive, he didn't want to risk attracting any attention. Besides, Sharon has been really keen to come with him – it seemed like she had a real soft spot for hard men like him.

So Eddie and Sharon found themselves at Panama's Tocumen International – which Sharon later described as 'the smallest, most unassuming airport outside of an Indiana Jones movie'.

A solitary baggage handler pointed them in the direction of the taxi. Eddie slipped on his Ray-Bans and marched over to the exit, his ox-blood loafers slapping against the tile floor. Sharon clicked along behind him in her red, five-inch heels. With her low-cut top and white mini skirt she drew some glances from the line of waiting drivers, sitting in the sun sharing cigarettes and stories.

Climbing into the first taxi in the line, Eddie shouted 'Hotel Panama' to the driver, and they were off. They made their way towards Panama City, and saw the looming multitude of residential and corporate high-rises. Eddie was no stranger to these shores, which became self-evident when he was greeted enthusiastically by the hotel porters. They were there, as Eddie constantly reminded Sharon, for business, so after a quite bite to eat, they went straight upstairs to bed. Eddie had been a surprised at Sharon's insistence that they have separate rooms… but then women were always a bit of a mystery to him.

'I don't care where you sleep,' he had told her. 'Suit yourself.'

They were up at the crack of dawn. After a hurried breakfast, Eddie led Sharon through the narrow streets of Panama City. Sharon, who had said that she never been out of Europe before, was especially taken by the Kuna Indian women, and their traditional, brightly-coloured 'socks', worn from the ankles up to their calves, with strands of tiny red and orange beads forming traditional geometric designs. Every time they passed, in their dark blue and yellow skirts and peasant style blouses, decorated across the front and back with fabric paintings, she would pull out her camera... which Eddie was finding increasingly annoying.

More as a means of control, rather than affection, Eddie eventually took Sharon's hand and led her deeper into the back streets. He was, she noticed, taking an unusual interest in the Indian woodcarvings.

'Come on, Ed,' she moaned, 'this is so *boring*. Let's get on with your deal, then we can relax.'

But this was one meeting that Eddie would not be accompanied to. No matter how many times Sharon said that she'd be scared to be on her own, he insisted that he was going on alone. Eventually, she gave in. Eddie pulled out a thick wad of dollar bills from his pocket, peeled off ten fifties, and told her to go and buy some souvenirs for her friends back home. He watched her leave. *Thank Christ for that, some peace and quiet.* She might have been a friendly face around the office, someone he enjoyed flirting with, but he was finding that being with her 24/7 was getting on his nerves.

Navigating the winding back streets in a low-income neighbourhood, Eddie made his way to a small local bar that smelt of stale cigarettes and cheap Seco. His contact, a stern-faced native, was there already, waiting to escort him to the warehouse. They shook hands, and the contact immediately led Eddie to an ancient, battered hatchback parked haphazardly nearby.

Driving further away from the tourist area, deeper and deeper into the bowels of the government housing and squatter slums, they finally pulled up outside a grimy warehouse. Once inside, Eddie was totally mesmerised by the dangerous-looking men, immersed in their work... impregnating sheets of plywood with liquid cocaine.

The plywood would then be incorporated into elaborate doors, decorated with carvings of green parrots – and sent overseas. It was an ingenious system, and Eddie was keen to try it out.

Eddie ordered and paid for the UK delivery of 12 of these cocaine-laced doors, for the equivalent of just over £3,000 each. *Bargain*, Eddie thought, as they closed the deal with a handshake.

'You wouldn't Adam and Eve it!' Eddie laughed, almost choking on a mouthful of cherry cake. 'When the doors were delivered by TNT, Sylvia was clobbered for eight hundred quid importation tax! She only paid it with her Visa card. She had the right hump, and told the delivery driver to load them in the garage. She hadn't got a Scooby! I told her that we were refurbishing a gaff in Bayswater, the dozy twonk!'

Eddie told Johnny how, once the doors had arrived, he had them picked up from his home in St John's Wood by a hired white Transit van, and taken to the arches under London Bridge. Plastic sheeting was used to create a quarantine area, and four South American associates, wearing white decorator's suits and face masks to protect against the toxic fumes, started to extract the cocaine.

In Central America this was all done in the open air, but in the middle of London, that just wasn't an option. The doors were split into three-foot lengths for easy handling, then the surface rasped and grated into a pile of shavings. The fine shavings were then placed into 45-gallon drums containing industrial solvent, and heated to separate the wood from the cocaine. Once dry, they would be left with approximately 17.2 kilos of pure cocaine, in powder form. And once this was cut with other substances, and tripled in weight to around 52 kilos, it would be worth more that £1.5 million on the street.

Johnny, Eddie and Hate-'em-all-Harry simultaneously leaned back on their chairs, their chests puffed with pride, knowing smiles plastered across their faces.

A burly prison guard stood up, and called, 'End your visits please.'

As Hate-'em-all and Eddie got up to leave, Eddie winked at Johnny.

'You never know, Johnny,' said Eddie, pulling down his cuffs. 'As Del Boy says, "a year from now, we could be millionaires".'

twelve

Stella Evans was a director with a vision. Although Rosie might not have had the experience of most of the other actors who had been cast in *My Fair Lady*, one thing she did know was that it was unusual to film entirely on location. That said, the magnificent Edwardian house on Berkley Square, where the cast and crew had all met for lunch, was so enormous that it almost looked as if it had been designed as a film set. Rosie had already seen pictures of it, and read about it in the publicity hand-outs, but the scale and splendour of the place was so thrilling that it made her swell with pride to see it. The set designers and dressers had evidently been hard at work, as many of the rooms were completed, ready for filming to commence. Elsie, the publicist, was dashing around directing everyone to the kitchen where caterers had an impressive array of refreshments waiting.

As everyone milled around, sipping tea and munching triangle sandwiches, Rosie wandered thought the maze of rooms with Thomas R Williams, who, it emerged, was also seeing the location for the first time. Rosie was becoming rather fond of Tom, as he had insisted she called him. Despite being one of England's most established actors, he was completely approachable and, as anyone who had seen him on television or at the cinema would expect, immensely charming.

'It's wonderful, isn't it?' she murmured, as they strolled around the drawing room, lined with panelled walls and tall bookcases, crammed with gold-bound first editions.

'I've never seen anything like it,' Tom replied, genuinely awe-struck, adding, 'how are you feeling about tomorrow?' as they sat down on a buttoned Chesterfield sofa.

After some consideration, Rosie replied, 'I think I'm ready to get started. How about you?'

'Same,' he smiled. With his thin pale face and fine black hair, he really was incredibly handsome. 'If there's time later, I'm happy to quickly run through our lines.'

'I'd love to, thank you,' said Rosie, touched by his offer.

'Ah!' exclaimed Elsie, clapping her hands together as she flew into the room. 'Here you are.'

Tom gave an enigmatical raise of one eyebrow.

'We are about to tour the house, are you coming?'

Tom stood up, offered Rosie his arm, and they gracefully stepped into the hall to join the rest of the actors and key members of the crew.

After the final briefing was over, Rosie was heading

towards her chauffeured ride home when the security barriers rose up. A sleek, black Range Rover drove in, and pulled up alongside her. Rosie smiled as the smoked glass window on the driver's side smoothly rolled down; she already knew who it was.

'Can I give you a lift home?' Andrew Brook-Fields offered.

'Great timing,' said Rosie, and tugged open the passenger door.

On the journey home, Andrew listened with amused interest as Rosie rattled on about the Berkley Square location. It wasn't until they pulled into Hewitt Way that she realised that she had talked so much that she had hardly paused for breath. Feeling her cheeks start to burn, she turned and looked at Andrew. As he pulled up the handbrake, his eyes focused on Rosie. They were swimming with an intensity that she couldn't fathom. Her face flushed beet red as her stomach did a violent flip, and as her gaze wandered to his lips, she actually began to feel dizzy. The tension was finally broken by Andrew, leaning forward and pecking Rosie on the cheek. His lips felt warm and spongy.

'Good luck for tomorrow,' he whispered gently.

'Thank you,' mumbled Rosie.

'You'll be fantastic!' he said, giving her hand a gentle squeeze.

Rosie smiled, slightly awkwardly, opened the door, and got out.

'Let's speak again in the week,' said Andrew, as he started up the car.

That night, too excited and nervous to sleep, Rosie lay in her room, reading and re-reading her lines. She eventually managed to close her eyes for a few hours, and awoke with the confidence that she had, at least, the lines for her first day completely down.

The following morning, at precisely seven o'clock, Rosie stepped onto the set. Evidently, the crew had all risen much earlier to make a six o'clock start, as the house and grounds were a hive of activity. Rosie followed an enthusiastic runner – a girl called Nicky in her mid-twenties who had frizzy hair and trendy glasses – through a double swing door, into a courtyard, where a brand-new Winnebago was parked behind the main house. This was the first job in which she had a designated trailer, and she was quite taken aback to find that it was so plush. It was equipped with a corner sofa, angled around a square, glass coffee-table, a small fridge, and a make-up table with a large mirror, surrounded by lights, underneath which were several large bouquets of flowers. A large plasma screen covered almost the entirety of one of the walls, and a hanging rail was fixed on the wall opposite, crammed with various costumes in protective, plastic jackets.

'There's coffee and tea in there,' Nicky said, pointing to a pair of small flasks on a sideboard. 'If you want a full breakfast, you can get that in the kitchens in the main house. That's where the caterers are set up.'

'And the loo?' Rosie asked, faintly.

'Oh, yeah. There's one right through here,' she informed her, pushing open a door that was partly obscured by the loaded clothes rail. 'Shower, wash basin and WC, okay? Your personal dresser, and hair and make-up will be with you in a jiffy. I'll leave you now to get ready, but I'll be back to collect you for first call. Give me a shout if you need anything, okay?'

After Nicky had left, Rosie looked around her flashy trailer. *Wow!*. This is what she'd been waiting for, for years – it was her first step to becoming herself again. Her first step to becoming someone respectable. She carefully lay down her script on the coffee table. Thank goodness, she thought, that the first scene they were filming was just her and Tom. She already knew that she'd enjoy working with him, and so that really took the pressure off.

Rosie turned her attention to the huge bouquets of flowers by the mirror. She bent over them and her nostrils were at once filled with their heavy fragrance.

She examined the first bunch – a hand-tied, delicately scented freesia and nine, large-headed roses. Each stem had been expertly positioned, and the bunch had been tied with a pink ribbon. She opened the card – 'Good luck, Mummy! Love you – Ruby, Aunt Madge and Dibble.' Holding the flowers close, she inhaled a deep breath and smiled. The next bouquet was a fragrant and feminine arrangement of elegant Oriental lilies. The card read, 'Go, girl. Lol, Stevie.'

The stylish black vase on the brightly-lit dressing table contained what must have been close to 50 large-headed, deep red roses. She opened the small card, and read its simple message: 'Love you. Johnny.' Her heart sank. She didn't want anything for him any more.

But then she noticed, next to the stool in front of the dressing table, an exquisite bouquet of enchanting, pure-white Calla lilies. Rosie felt her heart jump... and not because they were her favourite flowers, but rather because she guessed immediately who they were from.

Sure enough, the card read, 'Make me proud, Andrew x.'

thirteen

For the ordinary man, being sent to prison is the most disorientating event they will probably ever experience. In one cruel swipe, every routine, every material comfort, and every friend and family member is suddenly whipped away from them. For most men, it's like being suddenly transported to another planet. But not for Johnny Mullins.

For Johnny, prison was just an inconvenience, a hazard of the job. For him, it was just a matter of pushing his cushy lifestyle to the back of his mind, and concentrating on his new reality. Right from the start he was determined that this new world, with its different noises and different smells, would not turn him into 'just another inmate'.

For most convicts, from the moment they enter prison they don't have to think for themselves. They are told exactly what to do and exactly when to do it. Some are, actually, very suited to this regimented existence, and find themselves comfortably morphing into robots. But for Johnny it was still a dog-eat-dog world, just like it was on the outside. After all, it doesn't take a genius to work out that if you lock a thousand men into one building for years on end, it's going to be like a bomb waiting to go off.

HMP Maidstone might have been full of hard-nosed cons, but as soon as a prisoner arrived, it was in his interest to remember that all men are not created equal. There was a strict pecking order. Right at the bottom, there were the scumbag outcasts – the child molesters, the rapists – who no one wants to be associated with. A few rungs up from them were the middle-men – petty thieves and two-bob merchants, mostly. They weren't scumbags exactly, but they weren't tough guys either. In fact, they were insignificant. The further up the ladder, the more complex the hierarchy became. But, at the top, it was the 'governors' that ran the prison – the murderers, the bank robbers... in short, the gangsters. But, above everyone, was Johnny Mullins. He was the top dog, the daddy. He ran the jail, and everyone inside knew that.

Not that that was much comfort for him. After five years inside, life for Johnny had become tedious and monotonous, and he was becoming increasingly short-tempered. The slightest incident could send him into a rage. Sure, he was the big cheese – he wouldn't have it any other way – he was the muscle, and he had complete control of the drugs that were dealt on the inside, but he was also fed up to the back teeth with prison life. Every day on C Wing was just like the one before, and just the same as the one that would follow it. Nothing *ever* changed.

The main event of the day, breakfast, had just started. Johnny stood on the landing, leaning over the hand rail, watching the inmates jostling for position, as they waited to be served their fry-up... if you could even call it that. He never had to queue for anything or anybody, as his food was normally delivered to his cell. But today there had been some delay or other in getting the hotplate onto the wing, and, as the time allocated for breakfast was nearly over, the prisoners were getting agitated.

'Get a fucking move on!' one of the prison guards shouted. He shoved a prisoner in the back, hard, and watched him fall against the con standing in front of him.

'What the fuck are you doing?' yelled the second man. 'You've made me drop my sausage!'

The sausage rolled across the filthy floor, picking up dust and ash in its grease, before coming to a halt amongst a collection of cigarette butts. Johnny watched in amusement as the man held out his tray for another one.

'That was the last one,' said the officer serving, 'there aren't any more.'

A deathly silence fell along the line.

'What? No more sausages?' someone gasped.

'I ain't 'aving that!' said the con. 'I'm *entitled* to a sausage, and I *want* my sausage. I want it *now*!'

The officer who had started this whole debacle,

who was now leaning against a wall and chatting, looked over and snapped, 'Never mind about your sausage. Move along.'

But the con was not giving up. 'I ain't fucking moving. I know my rights,' he sneered, banging his tray on the hot plate.

Things were turning ugly. Johnny had seen full-blown riots blow up over less. But, as he watched from the safety of the landing, he knew that none of the inmates would dare start anything without his say so. They knew better than that… and so did the guards. In a strange reversal of fortune, Johnny had found himself in the role of peacekeeper. Sure enough, one of the officers looked up at Johnny, as did the cons. Johnny shook his head and the message was clear: 'Leave it'.

Johnny walked slowly and deliberately along the landing, down the wrought iron staircase, and towards the hotplates. As he approached, everyone moved out of his way. He walked up to a particularly mean-looking inmate – Dominic, who had arrived less than a month ago and was in for GBH. He very slowly picked up the sausage from Dominic's metal tray, all the time staring him in the face. Then he turned, and handed it to the disgruntled con. For a full minute, no one said a word. Johnny looked into the faces of his fellow prisoners, daring them to challenge him, but nobody uttered a word. No one had the bottle.

Closing the door to his cell behind him, Johnny went over to his bunk, sat down, looked around at the four grey walls, and sighed. He thought back to how everything had gone so wrong, and how he had ended up in prison in the first place.

Years ago now, on a trip to Las Vegas, Eddie and Johnny had been introduced to a drug cartel called the Sinaloa, which came from an area in Mexico notorious for its gangsters. They had quickly struck a deal and, in no time at all, they were flying huge shipments of cocaine from Mexico to the south of Spain. From there, the powder was transported to Essex by light aircraft.

These planes flew in the shadow of the commercial flights around Stansted Airport, and, because of their size, were undetected by radar. Once they were above the Essex countryside, parachutists would exit the plane, free falling to the ground at speeds in excess of 125miles an hour. Strapped to each jumper was their precious cargo of between 30 and 40 kilos of pure cocaine. The 'Halo Club' – as the brothers had dubbed the parachutists – were all ex-military, but nevertheless a jump from 10,000 feet, without oxygen, and deploying the canopy at the last minute, was still extremely dangerous. Johnny and Eddie used this method for years, and these occasional drops had netted them a small fortune.

Then, one night, the parachute of one of the jumpers, Marcus King, failed to open properly and, spiralling out of control, he was sent crashing into an electricity pylon, knocking out electricity for much of Billericay and the surrounding area. Due to the excessive weight of cocaine that the brothers had insisted they carry, the unfortunate jumper broke his back, along with his cheekbone, right shoulder, three ribs, and two fingers on his right hand.

Not wanting to spend the next decade in prison, the recently-disabled parachutist turned supergrass, and sang like a canary. Both Johnny and Eddie were implicated, but Johnny decided that it made no sense for them both to go down – after all, *someone* had to run the business – so he took the rap.

In the hope of getting a reduced sentence – if you can call 18 years a reduced sentence – Johnny pleaded guilty to drug importation. After all, Johnny told himself, with good behaviour, he'd probably be out in eight to nine. Pulling in every favour that they could, and paying £250,000 in backhanders, Johnny got down-graded from a double A-category inmate to simply A-cat.

But 18 years is still 18 years and, although he'd already served five, Johnny was feeling the pressure. To make thing worse, he was bombarded with radio, television and press reports about Rosie's role in the forthcoming series of *My Fair Lady*. He loved her. He'd always loved her. He might not have always known it, but being inside has the effect of stripping away all the superficial crap in life, and leaves you with just the essentials for comfort. So Johnny's feelings for Rosie, and of course dear little Ruby, had become something of an Achilles heel.

Now, five years down the line, the only thing Johnny wanted, the only thing he really craved, was normality. He wanted Sunday afternoon barbecues, to mow the lawn, and to look up at night and see the stars. He wanted to feel Rosie's warm embrace. He wanted to see Ruby grow up. He wanted a family Christmas. In short, he wanted all the things he used to have but never appreciated.

Looking at the picture of Rosie on the pin board above his bed, Johnny sighed. The sound was so pitiful, he felt suddenly angry. *Pull yourself together*, he said out loud.

Then another gruff voice spoke inside his head. It was his Eddie's.

'One and a half *million* quid.'

Funny how quickly thoughts of cutting the grass, Sunday barbeques, and a family Christmas could disappear. £1.5 million worth of liquid cocaine did that for Johnny.

fourteen

Two days into filming, Rosie had her first day off. Andrew called to invite her to dinner, to discuss the rushes, the first rough edits of the footage that had been shot. Rosie's immediate reaction was that she must have done something wrong, that she wasn't good enough, and Andrew was going to tell her that they were going to re-shoot... or, worse still, re-cast.

It was just after eight when Rosie walked into the restaurant on the Fulham Palace Road in southwest London. A grand piano was the focus of the seating area, and with its pitched ceilings and large windows, the restaurant had an unusual, but undeniably welcoming feel. Rosie looked over at the kitchen, in full view in the back of the room, where large bowls of dough and sinks of ice holding the catch of the day were proudly on display. Next to them stood wooden-topped tables, floured and prepared to roll and cut fresh pasta, and baskets of fresh mushrooms ready for trimming. *I could get used to this*, Rosie said to herself.

Rosie handed the maître d' her coat, and turned to see Andrew winding his way through the tables, his eyes fixed on her. She suddenly felt breathless and shaky.

'Rosie!' Andrew said warmly, reaching out and taking her hands. He kissed her on both, reddening cheeks, before leading her to their table.

'A glass of champagne?' he offered, as the maître d' seated them.

'Lovely, thank you.'

The maître d' nodded his approval, and scurried off to get their drinks.

Rosie looked around admiringly. 'This is a wonderful place,' she said. 'I haven't been here before.'

'It's one of my favourites,' Andrew told her.

A slightly uncomfortable silence was eventually broken by Rosie. 'You said you had something to discuss?'

For a moment, it appeared as if he couldn't remember. 'Yes, of course,' he finally said, sitting up a little straighter.

'Is it about the rushes?' asked Rosie, in a nervous whisper. 'Is that what you wanted to talk about?'

He nodded thoughtfully. After the champagne had been delivered, he leaned forward, rested his elbows on the table, and in a low and intimate tone said, 'The rushes were fantastic, absolutely wonderful.'

He raised his glass and looked into Rosie's emerald-green eyes. 'Congratulations again.'

'Thank you, Andrew. I can't tell you how relieved I am to hear you say that.'

'Here's to you... and Eliza Dolittle.'

'To Eliza,' said Rosie, feeling a swell of pride, tossing her hair to the left.

As the first sip of the deliciously cold champagne touched her lips, Rosie felt almost drunk with relief that there wasn't a problem with her performance. Her mood had instantly changed, and she was suddenly aware of how lucky she was to be sitting in such a sophisticated restaurant, with such a wonderful, sophisticated man. This had been Rosie's dream for so long, and now that she was living it, it felt *so* right. She could hardly remember the last time that something had felt this good.

This was such a welcome change, Rosie thought, to Johnny and his Neanderthal ways. A good night out to him, she recalled, was a trip to the local steak house for a 16-ounce rib eye steak, washed down by a couple of bottles of house wine and half-a-dozen vodka and tonics... 'VATs', he used to call them. And as for the company – Eddie and sometimes Hate-'em-all – this was so refreshing. She shuddered at the recollection.

'There is another reason,' said Andrew, 'why I asked you here for dinner tonight. I think you've handled the press very well, and I'd like to think that the publicist dealt with your "revelations" professionally.'

Rosie nodded in agreement.

'Well, if I was your agent, I'd say that now is the time to start raising your profile, both professionally and personally. To make the most of this opportunity, it's important that you're seen in the right places, with the *right* people.' Andrew's eyes darkened slightly. 'If I can be so bold, that means no more bad boys.'

Andrew was cut short by the arrival of the maître d', armed with menus and the wine list. Rosie looked down and saw, to her horror that the menu was written entirely in Italian. She was suddenly completely out of her depth.

Reading her expression, Andrew intervened. 'I know the menu quite well. May I be bold, and order for both of us?' he asked. 'I recommend the Lobster Thermidor. It's really wonderful.'

She nodded, trying to hide her embarrassment. Andrew, in what sounded to Rosie like fluent Italian, gave their order.

'I've ordered a Chablis. I hope you approve,' he added, once the maître d' had left.

'So, tell me about you,' Andrew asked, making Rosie laugh. 'If that's not too old a line.'

'I think most of my life has been covered in the papers,' she said. 'But, if you insist…'

'I do.'

'Well, as you know, I have an estranged husband – more "strange" than "estranged", actually – serving 18 years in one of Her Majesty's finest. I was brought up by my aunt, Madge, who has a crazy dog called Dibble. And I live with the apple of my eye, my beautiful 12-year-old daughter, Ruby.' Rosie dug into her handbag, and smiled as she passed a photo over to show Andrew. His eyes sparkled and he couldn't suppress a smile as he gazed down at the picture.

'This could almost be you,' he told her. 'She is a dazzling beauty, destined to turn heads. Just like her mum.'

Bursting with pride, Rosie took the photograph back and slipped it into her handbag.

'That's pretty much all there is, I'm afraid' she said. 'Does that make me very boring?'

'Not in the least!'

'But I know nothing... nothing *at all* about you. Apart from a wife and two children.'

Andrew took a deep breath before answering. 'Sophie, my ex-wife, is a wonderful woman. In a way, I suppose, I'm still in love with her,' he said, in a matter-of-fact tone. 'But, as you know, things happen. Lives drift apart, and things change. It's the loss of the children that I miss most.'

'I'm so sorry' said Rosie, reaching out and giving his hand an encouraging squeeze.

'No... no, no. It's fine, really,' said Andrew, taking a moment to compose himself. Okay, they weren't mine by birth, but I brought the girls up as if they were. But now, as their mother and I are no longer together, she thinks it's best if they focus on building a relationship with her new boyfriend... while they... forget all about me.'

'No!' Rosie was horrified.

'I miss them terribly.'

'I can't believe a mother could *do* that. How old are they?'

'Amy is nearly 17 – she wants to be a photographer -- and Marianna is almost 15.'

'The same age as Ruby, give or take a year,' said Rosie.

Her heart really went out to Andrew. How could Sophie use the girls as a weapon against such a decent man?

Their conversation, which had become very intense in a very short space of time, was interrupted by the arrival of two spectacular dishes.

'Oh my God!' exclaimed Rosie, looking down at her food. She had never eaten lobster before, and she desperately wanted to make a good impression. Deciding that the most sensible route to take was to simply copy what Andrew did, she watched as he confidently brandished what looked like a silver nutcracker, and deftly tore off a pincer. Moments later, and somehow with his hands not covered in sauce, Andrew was tucking in.

Unable to continue the pretence, Rosie laughed out loud.

'That's it,' she cried. 'I think I've actually turned into Eliza Dolittle! I haven't got a clue what I'm eating, or how to go about it. Tell me, Andrew, did Stella bet you that you couldn't make me pass as a lady?'

Andrew looked across at her, and a sympathetic smile grew on his face. Putting down his fork and 'nutcracker', he sat back, dabbing the corners of his mouth with a white linen napkin.

'I am so… utterly thoughtless,' he said, apologetically, 'Oh, Rosie, can you ever forgive me? I didn't think, for one moment… I'm so sorry.'

'Is this art imitating life… or life imitating art? Oh, you know what I mean!' Rosie laughed and, in turn, so did Andrew.

'Well, it's good casting, at least... what with you being the real Eliza Dolittle,' he said.

From that moment on, the ice was broken between them. A mutual understanding was established. The evening continued in a flirtatious haze of champagne and Chablis. They enjoyed easy conversation, one topic flowing naturally into another, covering life, love, and expectation. Rosie found Andrew fascinating – well-read, broad-minded, but always interested in what she had to say. She had never met such an enigmatic, intriguing man in her life. He spoke five languages – Italian, French, Cambodian, Vietnamese, and Thai – he had business interests all around the world, and he knew absolutely *everyone* in the TV world.

After the meal, Andrew ordered a car to take them to their respective homes. On the way he explained that he wouldn't be visiting the set for a while, as he had to go to Asia, scouting for locations for a new drama set during the Second World War.

'I'll be pretty much incommunicado, I'm afraid,' he said. 'The phone networks are just terrible there. Still, I'm sure there won't be any slacking off on set, not with Stella around.'

'How long will you be gone?' asked Rosie, looking lazily out at the wet streets as they drove east.

'I not sure, but I suspect three weeks.'

'Oh, three weeks? That long?' After the words came out, Rosie wished that she hadn't said anything. The evening had gone so well, she didn't want to ruin the perfect atmosphere they had created by appearing even slightly possessive.

When the car stopped under the dim street lights of Hewitt Way, Andrew got out to open Rosie's door. After a non-committal peck on the cheek, as they stood face to face, the atmosphere was electric. Rosie longed for Andrew to scoop her up in his arms, and hold her in a long, lingering embrace. But she knew it wasn't to be – Andrew was too polite, too well mannered. He was a rare find – a true gentlemen.

That night, Rosie lay in her bed, engulfed in a warm and unfamiliar feeling. She was, perhaps for the first time in her life, on the threshold of something really special, really pure. As she drifted off into a deep contented sleep. She could only hope and pray that Andrew felt the same way,

A relentless ringing dragged her out of a sleep so deep that it took her a moment to register where she was. Eventually, Rosie rolled out of bed and stumbled downstairs, shaking her head, yawning, and wondering who would be calling her in the middle of the night. *Andrew?*

Rosie lifted up the receiver. 'Hello?' she mumbled.

'Rosie?' She should have known... she recognised the voice at the end of the line straight away. 'I *love* you, Rosie.' Johnny was slurring.

Johnny hadn't called in the middle of night for a while. Rosie was all too aware that this wouldn't be the last time, either, and that she'd have to start unplugging the phone before she went to bed. It meant that Johnny had a new mobile phone, one that someone had smuggled into the prison, probably wrapped in cling film and hidden in some con's backside.

'This time next year, Rosie, we'll be millionaires.'

Trust him to rain on her parade like this, Rosie thought as she felt her stomach tighten. He had no manners, no airs or graces – he was the polar opposite to Andrew. She had no feelings for him any more, apart from hatred and disgust. When would it end? How could he *still* disrupt her life like this, he was put away for 18 years, for God's sake.

Rosie hung up, turned off the lights, and made her way back up the stairs. At least they weren't living together any more, so she was free to do what she wanted, more or less. That hadn't really meant much before, but now there was something that she wanted… or, rather, some *one* – Andrew.

fifteen

Standing in her trailer, gazing out over the Edwardian London street scene, Rosie wondered if they would be able to shoot with so much mist – well, dry-ice – hanging thickly in the air. But it did look amazingly authentic. It was obvious that Stella was delighted with it. It was, she had said, just the environment that she imagined Eliza emerging from, through the fog, clutching her basket of flowers. Rain had been forecast later in the day, and the crew were intermittently looking up apprehensively at the looming clouds. Time was of the essence.

Becky, a friendly, middle-aged woman from Wardrobe, handed Rosie a basket of flowers and straightened her costume.

'You look *fantastic*,' she said. 'You'll be great.'

Rosie didn't share Becky's confidence. Everyone was depending on her, and the enormity of her responsibility was weighing heavy on her shoulders. She had hoped that, after filming for a few days, the nerves might have eased off… but it wasn't the case.

'Okay, I'll be back in five minutes,' said Becky, giving Rosie's arm an encouraging squeeze. Just then, Rosie's mobile rang.

'Hey, Mum,' Ruby chirped, 'how's it going?'

'I'm still in my dressing room. I'm still so nervous, Rube. I'm going to pieces. I don't know how to put myself back together.'

'Okay, okay, Mum. Do like I said – deep breaths, think of England.'

Rosie laughed. She already felt better. 'You know what? You're just what I need to keep me grounded. Thank you, darling.'

'No problem. That's what daughters are for! Seriously though, Mum, you'll be fine when they start rolling. You always are. I'm really rooting for you, you know? We all are. Here, Aunt Madge wants to talk to you.'

Rosie smiled. She felt so lucky to have such a considerate family.

'Now, I don't want any more of your nonsense, my girl. You can stop those nerves this instant. You're a talented actress, remember? They wouldn't have cast you if they didn't think you were up to the job.'

'I was just having a funny five minutes. I think I'm past it now. I call you later, okay? I've got to get going.'

'Well, good luck! Or "break a leg", or whatever I'm supposed to say.'

No sooner were the garter straps fastened to her boots, than Rosie was taken through for a final check of her make-up.

'You look wonderful!' Tom R Williams said, as Rosie arrived on set. 'Let's just hope the weather holds off, so we can get this one in the can. It would really be a shame to get all dolled up for nothing.'

Holding out his arm, he led her across the street to join a small group of extras. Finally, it was announced they were going for a take. The first assistant director called for quiet, and silence descended over the set. You could have heard a pin drop.

'Speed... turn over...' The cameras started to roll. The clapper boy snapped the board shut. 'And... action.'

Rosie's heart fluttered with a wonderful sensation of pride, mixed with nerves and elation. This was beyond anything she had ever dared to imagine. For a few seconds, nothing seemed to be happening. Then the camera began tracking across the scene, until it finally came to a halt, focusing on Rosie.

'Wanna buy some flowers, guv'nor?'

Rosie counted to three, and gently raised her head to lock eyes with Tom.

'And cut,' came the voice again.

'You were sensational,' Tom said to Rosie. 'I predict you'll be a star before the year is out.'

'No pressure, then,' Rosie laughed.

'Well done, everyone,' Stella announced, cracking a rare smile. 'Right, let's push on. There's still a lot to get through today.'

By the time the day's shoot was over, Rosie was exhausted. One drawback of having such a major part, she had discovered, was that she was spending almost every day on set. It wasn't the actual acting that was tiring, but more the endless standing around while lights and camera were set up.

Back in her dressing room, Rosie's phone beeped a familiar sound. She went to the inbox and opened the text, which read: 'Back in London weekend. Got 2 tickets for opera, *La Bohème*. Would love you to join me, A x.'

Rosie's heart skipped a beat, and she instantly typed her reply, 'Yes please!' Then it dawned on her: a trip to the opera? She really *was* turning into Eliza Dolittle.

For the next few days Rosie had something else, apart from the pressure of filming, to worry about. Actually, the anticipation she felt about her trip to see La Bohème was something she hadn't experienced since her first date with Johnny, when she was just a teenager. Doubts and insecurities kept cropping up, and she lost count of the amount of times she came close to cancelling. She spent the hours in her trailer, between shots, both dreading and longing for the weekend to arrive. She wasn't the only excited one, either —Ruby was so thrilled you would think that she was going on a date herself. True to form, she was full of advice about what her mum should wear, say, and even think.

Finally, the big night arrived. Filming had run on a

little, so Rosie had precious little time to get ready after the driver had taken her home. Rosie kissed Ruby on the forehead and disappeared into her bedroom to get changed. Looking at her modest wardrobe, Rosie was still completely undecided about to what to wear. As she had never been to an opera before, she had asked for advice from anyone who would listen. 'Don't wear kitten heels,' someone had said. She had been told by Tom's personal assistant, 'Don't wear a long dress,' which was all well and good... until Stella had said 'Whatever you do, don't wear a *short* dress'. A girl in Wardrobe had said 'Wear black velvet', which seemed like sound advice, if a little old fashioned. She really hadn't a clue.

Rosie pulled out all her dresses and eventually settled on a mid-length black velvet dress, which seemed to tick all the boxes, although Rosie hoped that it wasn't too low cut. *Oh well*, she thought, *It will have to do.* For her feet, she opted for a pair of – slightly inappropriate? – Jimmy Choo stilettos that Stevie had given her for her birthday a few years earlier. After getting changed, she took a look at herself in the mirror. She so wanted to get it right and to make the right impression for Andrew. After all, she was going to La Bohème... *whatever that was!*

Then, for some reason Rosie couldn't fathom, her thoughts drifted back to Johnny. *You wouldn't catch* him *at the opera.* Johnny preferred the Tin Pan, a proper East End club, which had no frills or fancies, or wine-bar pretensions. There wasn't even a carpet or decent curtains, she remembered... just curling cigar smoke and an atmosphere you could cut with a knife. Still, the Tin Pan was always busy, buzzing with noise and packed wall-to-wall with blokes, all past their prime – pot-bellied and flat-nosed, most of them. They would huddle in groups, leaning on the bar or against walls, and let their mouths run away with themselves. They would drink cheap beer, and, every now and again, one of them would start re-enacting their glory days in the ring, or the last fight they had caught on TV. They would start bobbing and weaving, ducking and diving, and saying 'If only... ya shoulda seen it – he came at me with a right 'ook. He went down for eight, it oughta been...'

These blokes didn't have blood in their veins, they had pure testosterone. The memories made Rosie shiver. She hated the Tin Pan. She hated all of the men who went there, too old and fat for anything but verbal sparring, not that that stopped them from trying to outdo each other. They were just living in the past, with their 'could-have-beens' and 'might-have-dones'.

But, back then, Rosie didn't have much choice where she went. The Tin Pan was a regular haunt for Johnny, Eddie and Hate-'em-all, probably because they were seen as the top dogs whenever they walked in. It was always the same every week – as soon as they entered, a buzz would go around the club: *The Mullins are in*. Within minutes there was a seemingly endless stream of broad-shouldered blokes with noses as wide as double wardrobes, all coming to shake their hands and say hello. It was a place where Johnny and Eddie felt good, among their own kind.

Thank God, Rosie said to herself, that she never had to go back to the Tin Pan.

Arriving at the magnificent Royal Opera House, tucked away in a corner of Covent Garden, Rosie was bowled over by the stunning architecture. Andrew was there to meet her and, taking his arm, they made their way inside. They were shown to their seats in the stunning, horseshoe-shaped auditorium, and Rosie looked around to see what women *actually* wore to the opera. She need not have worried, as there was a wide range of fashions on show – everyone was dressed to the nines, peacocking around as if they were royalty.

Silence fell as the lights dimmed and the opera began. From the first bar, Rosie was enchanted. The sound was so powerful, yet gentle. She might not have had a clue what the characters were singing about, but the feelings it stirred in her were intense.

After the lights came up and the applause had died away, she turned to Andrew, with a tear in her eye.

'I know exactly how you feel. That's how I felt when I went to my first opera,' he said with a smile.

'That was incredible. I'm... lost for words.'

'Come on, Eliza Dolittle,' he grinned. 'Pull yourself together, and I'll take you for supper.'

sixteen

Rosie was looking forward to a lie-in the next morning, thanks to a break in the filming schedule. But the extra hours in bed were not to be – Ruby was up early, eager to hear every last detail about her date.

'Come *on*, Mum! What happened?' Ruby cried, jumping on Rosie's bed. 'So he's not here?'

'What time is it?'

'Nearly eight-thirty. I've been going off my *head* waiting to find out how it went. Come on, cough. Every last detail.'

'I swear,' said Rosie, trying to sit up, 'you are the world's most precocious child.'

'Have you got your nightie on, Mummy?' Ruby asked, pulling back the duvet.

'Yes!' Rosie said, exasperated, grabbing the duvet back. 'And will you get off me please, you're heavy.'

'Didn't he stay the night?' Ruby teased.

'What do you think I am? A lush?'

'Well, did you snog him then Mum? Come *on*.'

'Okay, I give up,' said Rosie with a sigh. 'It was a fabulous evening. I can't remember when I felt so relaxed with a man and… yes, all right, we kissed. But only outside in the car.'

'Oh my God!' squealed Ruby. 'Oh my *God*! Why didn't you invite him in?'

'Oh, for heaven's sake,' Rosie exclaimed. 'Well, I didn't want to seem too eager, did I? But you will be thrilled to hear that he is coming round later to take us all out to lunch. Yes, that includes Aunt Madge, too. I can't wait for you to meet him.'

As she watched her daughter laughing, a shiver of happiness ran straight through her. 'I know I've only seen him a couple of times but I already have such a good feeling about it. It's like… something that was out of kilter has just clicked back into place.'

'That means,' said Ruby, 'you have to divorce Dad and marry him.'

'You don't think you're getting a little bit ahead of yourself, do you?'

By the time Andrew came to pick them up, having already stopped to collect Madge, who was sitting comfortably in the back seat of his Range Rover, Rosie just couldn't stop smiling. After answering the door, without saying a word, Rosie looked deep into Andrew's dark eyes, and kissed him briefly on the lips… which prompted an audible cough from Ruby, who was standing in the doorway.

135

'Ah,' said Rosie, turning round, 'here she is. My mischievous daughter, Ruby.'

Ruby's blue eyes were shining as she eagerly looked up at Andrew. With her hair loose, like her mother's, and her lips shimmering with the same pink gloss, she looked almost as radiant.

'Pleased to meet you, madam,' Andrew told her, winking and affectionately shaking her hand.

Beaming with delight, Ruby looked for a moment as though she might throw her arms around him. But, in the end, she said just one word: 'Cool!'

'I think you are extremely brave, taking us all out,' said Rosie with a smile, 'particularly when you realise how raucous Aunt Madge can get after a couple of glasses of her favourite tipple.'

'I heard that!' Aunt Madge shouted, from inside the car. 'It's true! Just you wait until I've had a tot of whisky,' she said. 'I'm anybody's!'

'*Please* tell me she didn't just say that,' Rosie mumbled, as everybody started to laugh. She turned to her daughter, adding, 'And before you say one word, Ruby-two-shoes – whatever is on the tip of your tongue, swallow it!'

Ruby looked over at Andrew, who was clearly enjoying himself immensely.

'Is Dibble okay with you in the back, Aunt Madge?' Andrew asked, as they climbed into the car.

'She's fine and dandy, thank you.'

'Great,' he said, starting the engine. 'I've booked a table at The Swan. It's a quiet pub just opposite Hyde Park. That way we can have our lunch, and then walk Dibble. How does that sound?'

'That,' Aunt Madge replied, 'will suit me and Dibble lovely.'

Half-an-hour later they pulled up outside The Swan. Once Rosie, Aunt Madge and Dibble were out of the car, Ruby quickly hopped into the front seat and said, 'Can I come with you while you park?'

'Oh, leave him in peace, Rube,' said Rosie.

'It's okay,' said Andrew, clearly delighted. 'Right, seat belt on. Do you know this area at all?'

'Not really' said Ruby, giving her mother a cheeky wave as they pulled away.

'Well,' said Andrew, peering out of the windscreen and up a the sky, 'at least it's clear. We'll be able to go for a nice walk through Hyde Park with Dibble after lunch. I've heard all about her.'

'Hmm… you wait and see! She'll soon let you know if she likes you or not,' said Ruby.

After the car was parked they started back towards the pub, walking side by side in a slightly awkward, but pleasurable silence. As they prepared to cross the busy road, Ruby shyly took Andrew's arm.

'Mum told me that you don't see your stepchildren any more,' she said, letting go of him as they reached the other side. 'That's a shame. I expect you miss them, don't you?'

'Yes, I do,' he admitted.

'Do you think your wife may end up changing her mind?'

He inhaled deeply before answering. 'I would like to think so, but she isn't showing much sign of it yet, I'm afraid.'

'You'll keep trying though?'

'Of course.' He looked down at her, and smiled fondly. 'I hear you don't see much of your father. That's a great shame, too.'

Ruby shrugged. 'He was into drugs and stuff before he went away, so it's best I don't see him, really.'

'Don't you miss him?'

'No. Well, I suppose I do *a bit*. But he was always out of it and shouting at Mum, then passing out like he was in a coma. He wasn't very nice. So, actually, I was quite glad when he went away.' Ruby took a deep breath and lifted her shoulders up as high as she could, then let them drop – something she'd picked up from her mother. 'It's kind of funny, don't you think? That you don't see your children, and I don't see my dad. It's like, perhaps we can fill the empty spaces for each other, you know if you and Mum do get together. Think you will?'

Unable to stifle a laugh, Andrew said, 'It's certainly my hope.'

'What's so funny?'

'I was just thinking what your mum would say, if she could hear us.'

'I suppose I shouldn't have said that, should I?' said Ruby, looking up at him. 'Please don't tell her. She'll get all embarrassed and cross with me.'

'Don't worry it'll be our little secret.'

Ruby gave Andrew an affectionate punch on the arm. 'You're really cool,' she said.

'You're really cool, too,' he replied.

By the time they had finished lunch, the sun had broken through the clouds making the walk in Hyde Park a must. A gentle, fresh breeze rustled through the trees and, as ever, the park was packed with families, sweethearts and more than a few tourists.

Rosie, happily flushed with the warmth of a new romance, walked alongside Aunt Madge. Being outside, enjoying such a wholesome pleasure, made her remember that being a mother is all about savouring the simple things in life. And what could be better than taking a leisurely stroll in the autumn sunshine with your new boyfriend and your daughter? Andrew walked ahead with Ruby, who was holding onto Dibble's lead extremely tightly, just as Aunt Madge had told her.

'He's wonderful with her, isn't he?' Rosie said, wrapping her arms around Aunt Madge from behind as they walked.

Patting her hands, Madge said, 'Well, you kissed a lot of frogs before you found Prince Charming. It's about time your luck changed, my girl.'

'Can you ever imagine Johnny talking the dog for a walk in Hyde Park?' Rosie asked.

'No, not really. I always told you his eyes were too close together,' said Madge, looking over at the swans gliding across the Round Pond. 'Anyway, if Johnny did come, he'd bring along that big, ugly brother of his… and that Hate-'em-all-Harry. "Hate-'em-all" – I could never understand why he was called that.'

'Well, just look at him,' Rosie said. 'I think he does exactly what it says on the tin.'

'Anyway,' said Madge, 'I've never known Johnny to walk around Hyde Park playing happy families… this may be turning out to be precisely that.'

Rosie arched her eyebrows. 'Shut up! This is only our *second* date. Give us a chance, will you? *And*, in case you've forgotten, we are both still officially married.'

'At least dear little Ruby has taken to him… that's good,' Madge continued. 'We'll just have to wait and see what happens.'

As they continued to stroll down the curving paths, heading towards the Serpentine, they could hear the distant sound of a police siren.

'Listen, Rosie,' said Aunt Madge, 'they're playing Johnny's favourite tune.'

seventeen

Rosie stared at her mobile phone for a full minute before returning Eddie's call. He'd left a brief, stern voicemail message telling her — *no, ordering her* — to ring him back as soon as she could.

'Rosie?' he said, as soon as he'd picked up the phone. 'I need to see you tomorrow morning.'

'I can't, Eddie,' Rosie interjected, already regretting that she had phoned. 'I'm going to Bristol for a meeting.'

'No you're not,' said Eddie, as stubborn as ever. 'Be at the Chase Hotel at eleven-thirty. Don't be late.'

'Eddie, you don't —'

The phone went dead. Rosie knew that there was no point in calling back. She didn't have a choice. She could tell from the tone of Eddie's voice that he meant business and wouldn't take no for an answer. Her train from Paddington London left at four-thirty, and was due to arrive at Bristol almost two hours later. So if it all went according to plan, she could still meet Eddie and not upset her schedule.

The meeting in Bristol was one that she really couldn't miss. It was a get-together at Straw/Gold's main office to discuss publicity and promotion, followed by a dinner. All of the top people from *My Fair Lady* were going to be there, and it was the first really important get-together since filming ended a week ago.

At just after eleven the next morning, Rosie arrived at the Chase Hotel, an up-market, converted coaching inn from the 17th Century, set in some of the most beautiful countryside in Essex… and smack in the middle of the loads-of-money stockbroker belt. Looking at her watch, Rosie saw that she was early. After ordering a coffee and Danish pastries she took a seat by the window so she could see when Eddie arrived. She looked out over the impressive view – there was a dovecote on the lawn, a slow-moving trout stream, and rolling fields reaching out to the horizon. Rosie had been up since the crack of dawn and was in dire need of some caffeine, so when the coffee and pastries arrived they really hit the spot. But, still, she couldn't fully appreciate her breakfast or the beautiful surroundings – she was deep in thought as to why Eddie wanted to see her. *It had to be the Keyhole Club tape.*

Eventually, a silver Mercedes with the number plate EDM1 pulled into the courtyard, taking its place among the rows of expensive cars parked outside. Many of them, Rosie had noticed, contained saddles, gun dogs and golf clubs. Eddie lumbered out of the car and casually flicked the remote, locking the doors. *Yep, that's Eddie all right…* shoulders a mile wide, perfectly groomed hair, a serious, menacing face. He was alone – no Hate-'em-all-Harry – so Rosie knew that something was up.

Rosie watched him make his way inside. He looked very out of place there, she thought, surrounded by china cups, silver coffee pots, and crisp white tablecloths. He was turning some heads. People were giving him a wide berth, one man even pushing himself up against the wall as Eddie strode past. Not that Eddie noticed – he always moved slowly and deliberately, never side-stepping anyone. Spotting Rosie, he headed over to her, forcing a smile.

'Rosie, how are you?' he growled, holding out a hand the size of a dinner plate as he towered over the table.

From where she was sitting, Eddie looked bigger than she remembered. He had made an effort, covering his 17-stone – which was largely muscle – in a cashmere suit and a pale-blue silk shirt, and tie. Rosie thought back to what Aunt Madge had said once – 'You can dress a pig in a suit, but you won't stop it grunting!' As she got up and shook his hand, Rosie smelled a hint of aftershave, Davidoff Cool Water, which reminding her of Johnny. They always did dress alike, down to the obligatory chunky gold ring set with diamonds that sparkled on their little fingers. Rosie often wondered who copied who.   'Well, well, you're quite the little film star these days,' Eddie sneered, before calling over a waiter and ordering a freshly-squeezed orange juice and another coffee for Rosie.

'How's little Ruby?' Eddie asked, sounding genuinely interested.

Rosie was familiar with this quirk of Eddie's. He was a mass of contradictions – one minute he was polite and thoughtful and the next you'd catch a glimpse of all the pent-up fury that lurked beneath the surface, ready to explode. Rosie didn't know if he did it on purpose, to keep people on the back foot, or whether he wasn't aware that he was doing it at all. Either way, it worked. There was no way that anyone could second guess him.

'What do you want, Eddie? I've got a train to catch, so just get on with it,' she said.

'We need you to do something for us, Rosie'

For us. That meant 'for the business'. Rosie felt her insides freeze. 'Whatever it is Eddie, the answer is no.'

Eddie's eyes narrowed, and displayed the expensive veneers that he had got in California as he gritted his teeth. Rosie knew that he wasn't used to hearing 'no' from anyone... especially from a woman.

'"No" is not an option,' he hissed. 'We need someone we can trust, someone with your talents.'

'I'm not doing it.'

'You've done it before, and you'll do it again,' Eddie snapped. 'There's an associate, a "friend", inside on remand –'

'I know I did it before,' Rosie said, cutting him off, 'but I was young and dumb, and Johnny bullied me into it. But I wasn't happy about it then, and I'm not happy about it now. It's your sordid little world, not mine… not any longer. I've got myself straight, I move in different circles now, with decent people. I'm not about to jeopardise that. Not for you, Johnny, or anyone else.'

Eddie glared across the table at her. Rosie knew him well enough to see that his mask was beginning to slip.

'I am not asking you Rosie,' Eddie said slowly, pronouncing each little syllable carefully. 'I am telling you. And you will do what I tell you.'

Rosie looked into Eddie's unblinking eyes. He was terrifying when he was like this, capable of anything.

'Now,' he continued, his voice as quiet as a whisper, 'you fuck off and get your train to Bristol with your hoity-toity new pals, and you think about what I've told you. I'll be in touch.'

Rosie watched Eddie leave. She hated him so much she could almost taste it, hated everything he stood for… and hated his brother who brought her into their world. An old question screamed inside her head: 'How could you have ever fallen for such a man? *Loved* such a man?'

Eddie climbed into his car and drove out of sight. Her long-term connection to Johnny, which she had once considered to be a love knot, was still wrapped tightly around her… so tight, in fact, that Rosie was beginning to see it as a noose that would eventually strangle the life out of her.

The Great Western train to Bristol was on time. Rosie made her way to her seat, in a carriage at the far end of the platform. She couldn't remember the last time she had travelled first class – Straw/Gold, Andrew's production company, didn't do things by halves. She struggled to put her overnight bag in the luggage rack above the seat, and so turned to a fellow passenger for help.

'Of course,' the man said. 'No problem.' He had an unusually authoritative voice.

As her Good Samaritan forced the case into the rack, Rosie could smell stale cigarette smoke on him. Once it was safely stowed away, he nodded, sat back down on a nearby seat, and unfolded a copy of the *Financial Times*. Rosie stares at him – he looked familiar, but she couldn't place him. He was a balding, slightly portly man, with heavy jowls.

Was this Johnny's 'friend' on day home leave? Rosie could feel her throat tighten… was this man following her to deliver a message? She knew that there was no shortage of lowlife criminals who were so desperate to impress Johnny that they would do anything that he asked them to do.

Once they were on their way, Rosie noticed that the man was occasionally peering over the top of the salmon-pink broadsheet. On the third or forth time that he did this, she looked back… and he quickly averted his gaze. Then it hit her: he was the man from Joe Allen's, where she had gone for lunch with Andrew. Surely a con on day release wouldn't go to smart restaurant or travel in a first class carriage? Then it occurred to Rosie that this man could be an obsessive fan, a stalker who had read about her in the paper. That was marginally better than if he had been sent by Johnny, but it was still hardly a comforting thought.

As surreptitiously as she could, Rosie looked for clues to establish who the stranger was. She noticed that his blazer looked as if it had been bought off the peg for someone else, and he didn't look comfortable in it. And one of the turn-ups on his crumpled grey trousers was drooping towards a well-worn shoe… a very particular type of black leather shoe with an AirWair sole, and one that Rosie recognised. It was the type of shoe that was standard issue for police officers.

As the train hurtled away from smoky London towards the West Country, Rosie did her best to forget about the policeman… if that was, in fact, who he really was. She bought a black coffee and found her thoughts drifting back again to Eddie, and his 'request'. Was this why she was being followed?

Rosie would never forget the first time she truly realised the extent that she was involved in with the business. She was so ignorant back then, the enormity and seriousness of what she was doing simply didn't register with her. She was young and naïve, and just wanted to make Johnny happy.

It had all started when Hate-'em-all-Harry had phoned her, completely out of the blue. Rosie was immediately intrigued because he *never* called her… in fact, Hate-'em-all hardly ever spoke at all. His role in the brothers' firm was as confidant – he was Eddie and Johnny's ears and eyes –

and he was the only person they completely trusted. Hate-'em-all was a big man with small eyes set closely above a corrugated nose that stared with an unnerving intensity into a private world of hostility and hatred.

As his name suggested everything about Hate-'em-all spelled violence. His shoulders started underneath his chin, and spread outwards like a rugged mountain. Touch him, and he felt like he was sculpted from granite. Rosie hardly ever spoke to him, but over the course of that two-minute phone call she discovered that he didn't mince his words. He told her that she had to go and have her photograph taken, wearing a disguise.

Rosie had been very green back then, and she didn't ask any questions – she dutifully went to a photo booth at London Bridge Station and had the picture taken. She had treated it just like an acting job, and hadn't questioned Hate-'em-all's motives in any way. Unbeknown to her, the photo was then sent to a Dutch inmate, serving 25 years in Ley Hill open prison.

It emerged that Hate-'em-all had been writing to the prisoner for months, making out he was the girl in the photo, the inmate's girlfriend. Rosie was then ordered, by Johnny this time, to accompany him, Eddie and Harry on the journey to the prison in South Gloucestershire. She was made to visit the Dutchman, and relay a message – a date, a time, and a number – and that was it. Unbeknown to Rosie, the number referred to the part of the fence surrounding the prison, and the time and the date to when the inmate was to be sprung.

The day came, and Rosie made her way through the security checks – straightening her wig before looking into the security camera. It was only when she was shown into the visiting hall and told to wait that she realised that she had no idea what her 'boyfriend' looked like. Each time a prisoner came through the secure door, Rosie stood up. And, each time she realised that it wasn't him, she pretended to look for something in her pocket.

Eventually a short, Nordic-looking blond man with cruel eyes came through the door, and headed straight for Rosie's table. He didn't smile or say a word as he sat down, so Rosie went and collected two plastic cups of lemonade from the canteen's hatch. Another issue she hadn't considered was the language barrier. It emerged that the Dutchman spoke very little English indeed. This made conveying the message very difficult, especially as she didn't have a pen and paper, and did not want to arouse suspicion by asking for them. At long last, after 20 frustrating minutes, Rosie had finally got him to understand. Of course, once he had taken it in, she had no need to stay, and was eager to get out of the stinking visitors' hall. Rosie smiled as she remembered how she abruptly stood up, shouted at the Dutchman, slapped him around the face, and walked out. She'd seen enough arguments during visiting time to accurately recreate one.

Once she was outside, Rosie made her way to the car park and found the others. She climbed into the passenger seat next to Hate-'em-all-Harry. Eddie and Johnny, as usual, sat in the back. She pulled the wig off her head and stared directly ahead, trying to hold back the tears. Of course, she had known the day she married Johnny that she would have some connection to the criminal underworld. But, now she had seen the harsh reality of it she was desperate to avoid being sucked into it completely. It was then that she vowed never to do anything like that ever again.

But, looking back, Rosie knew that she had actively helped Johnny and Eddie before that trip to Ley Hill. They were very meticulous men, almost pedantic, and it was important to them to have every detail of every robbery carefully planned. In the early days of Rosie and Johnny's marriage, all the bank robbers, gangsters, thieves and thugs from their gang would regularly turn up at their home. Of course, Rosie was never allowed to overhear what was said on in her own front room – not that she really wanted to. She was always banished to the kitchen to make tea and sandwiches.

Rosie quickly learnt that a robbery is, in many ways, like staging a theatrical production. Certainly it's dramatic, and requires a great deal of attention to detail to make it convincing. In fact, in those early days Rosie would often feel as if she had been unwittingly cast in some crude crime drama. Just like in a play, Eddie and Johnny had to have the appropriate props to make their operation as effective as possible. They had acquired so many over the years that, eventually, they had their own prop store – a lock-up on an East London backstreet. It was packed with workmen's shelters (those red-and-white striped portable tents that electricians put up in the street – they could hide a couple of armed men, no problem); a whole range of costumes, such as reflective vests, street-sweepers' brooms, donkey jackets and boots; 'road closed' and 'diversion' signs to keep unwanted traffic out of the way; temporary bus-stop signs (in case there was a bus stop directly outside the bank, so passengers would queue away from the target – or for when they wanted to have someone 'queuing' outside, who was actually casing it).

Rosie had helped in her own way. She had her own prop store, with a whole range of wigs, hair dyes and false moustaches. As police and prison authorities kept careful records of a criminal's distinctive marks, like tattoos and scars, Rosie would use theatrical make-up and temporary tattoos. She would give the gang members new physical identities, including facial scars and tattoos on their hands and arms, for any witnesses to remember and report to the police. Rosie loved Johnny, and so wanted to please him that she did just what she was told, even if he was belittling her in front of his men. 'You're an out-of-work, frustrated actress, ain't ya?' Johnny would say. 'You can put all that training to some good use... now, give him a moustache, or dye his hair, or something.'

That was the reality of her married life back then – if Rosie wasn't making tea and sandwiches for the brutes in the lounge, she was putting tattoos, wigs, or false moustaches on them. That was what 'had to be done' when Johnny and Eddie were climbing the ladder to success. But it wasn't the life she had wanted for herself.

151

As the train passed Bath Spa, Rosie took a sip of her now-cold coffee, and considered how lucky she was to be out of all that... and to have never have been tried with aiding and abetting.

By the time the train lurched into the station at Bristol, Eddie's thinly-veiled threats were still echoing inside her head, and Rosie was finding it hard to focus on the important meeting ahead.

'Could you help me again?' Rosie asked her fellow passenger.

'Uh, yes. Of course,' he replied, clearly a little nervous at speaking to her directly.

After he had carefully taken Rosie's bag from the rack, Rosie gave him a smile.

'Thank you, Mr...?'

'Harris,' he said, after a telling pause.

'Are you following me?' she asked, her chin up and looking right at him.

'What makes you think that?' he said, defensively. 'No, of course not.'

'Oh,' she said, 'my mistake.' *Definitely a copper*, thought Rosie.

She had no problem finding a taxi outside the station, and was soon checking in at the hotel, a beautiful building that overlooked the rejuvenated waterfront. It emerged that Andrew – or, rather, his production company – had reserved the loft suite for her. It had a truly stunning bedroom, with a vast, comfy-looking bed with crisp, white, Egyptian-cotton sheets. The bathroom, with its luxurious twin baths, was large enough to play squash in. Looking at her watch she saw she was in good time for the meeting, so she selected Stevie's number on her mobile and pressed 'call'.

'I swear…' Rosie said, pulling open a set of French windows to take a look outside, before murmuring, 'Oh my God,' as she stepped onto the balcony that overlooked the courtyard. 'You should come here with Joe, Stevie, the next time you are over. You *have* to see this place.'

'I've no problem with that,' Stevie replied. 'So, are you meeting with Andrew tonight?'

'No, no. It's for work,' Rosie said. 'He said he probably won't be able to make it.' Just then, there was a knock at the door. 'Oh, hang on a minute, Stevie.'

Stevie waited patiently on the line, and listened while she heard Rosie thanking someone. Seconds later, she was back on the line.

'Okay… guess who *that* was?'

'No!' said Stevie, 'So he *did* make it. Funny that.'

'He just popped up to say hello, to touch base. We're meeting for dinner in the bistro downstairs later, at eight o'clock.'

Stevie giggled. 'This is it! This is it, girl! He's going to wine you and dine you… then he's coming back to your room!'

'Oi!' said Rosie. 'I can't believe you just said that! No, it's just work, okay? Just work… honestly. I've got to be professional.'

'Professional about what?'

'Stevie, stop it! As if!'

'Well, we'll have the same conversation in the morning then, shall we?' Stevie said, unable to contain her glee.

After saying their goodbyes, Rosie ran a bath and laid out her little black Gucci dress on the bed. Looking at its daring neckline and short hemline, she began to question whether it was appropriate for a dinner meeting. *Oh well*, she thought, *it's all I've got*.

After her bath, a final dab of perfume, and a critical glance in the mirror, she left the room, floated down the wide, sweeping staircase, and walked to the meeting at Straw/Gold's offices and production studios, which was just round the corner from the hotel.

The meeting, as expected, ran over. It was only after Tom and Sir Laurence James – who was well into his sixties and a big enough star to dictate anyone's schedule – started to complain, quite vocally, that Andrew wound it up.

Once they were back at the hotel, Rosie arched her eyebrows and smiled as she made her way through Roman-style pillars into the hotel's restaurant. The 30-strong party took their seats around a colossal table that had been especially arranged for them, and Rosie was delighted to find that she was sitting opposite Andrew. The evening passed in a haze of animated conversation, fuelled by vast quantities of champagne and wine. Towards the end of the meal, Rosie suddenly became aware of how flirtatious she and Andrew were being… she had hardly spoken to anyone else all night!

After dinner, as the cast and crew were saying their goodbyes, Andrew offered to walk Rosie to her room. Without saying a word, she took his arm, and they left together. As they reached the door, there was a brief, awkward moment. Rosie was full of trepidation. The only man she had ever slept with was Johnny, and if she invited Andrew in, she knew what was going to happen. Her heart was thundering with anticipation and she could feel her nervousness with each snatched breath. She was searching every corner of her brain for something to say, but could do nothing but stare. Eventually, Andrew spoke.

'You are so beautiful,' he said, studying her face. 'When I look at you, I find it hard to believe that you are here with me. I'm worried I'm going to wake up.'

Putting her arms tentatively around Andrew's neck, she pressed her mouth to his.

'Did that feel real?' she asked.

He nodded, and pulling her close. It was passionate but... gentle. Gentleness was not a quality that Rosie had really experienced before, so she was taken aback. But she knew then what would happen... she took Andrew by the hand and led him into her room.

Once inside, Andrew took control. He put his arms around her, and kissed her passionately as he undid her dress, letting it slip it off her shoulders. Rosie's inside tightened into a thousand knots. She hadn't slept with a man since Johnny was imprisoned. *Five years ago.* A tsunami of warmth engulfed her as Andrew laid her, naked, onto the bed. Rosie watched him undress, the sight of his body sending pulsing shivers down her tingling spine.

Their lovemaking was tender and loving. Andrew seemed to know how to please her in ways that she had never experienced. Being with him, there was an intimacy that she couldn't really understand. And afterwards, Rosie realised just what had been missing in her marriage to Johnny. He may have thought he was a good lover, but, in reality, he just fizzed around the bedroom like a sexed-up firework. Andrew's lovemaking, however, was sweet, tender and unselfish.

As she lay in his arms, looking into his dark eyes, he whispered, 'I don't know what happens from here, but whatever it is, I want us to be together.'

Rosie answered without hesitating: 'So do I.'

eighteen

For the following few weeks, Rosie was intoxicated with happiness. Her new relationship was growing stronger by the day and felt almost beyond her control. Although falling head-over-heels for someone had not worked out for Rosie in the past, it felt so right this time. After all, as she told Madge, she was basically a kid when she met Johnny. That said, she did feel like a teenager again – heady and giddy. The change in her was obvious to everyone, including the lady who served the tea at the local café. Of course, Stevie, Aunt Madge and little Ruby, were well aware of the cause.

Ruby was especially happy for her mum, and it was obvious that she liked having Andrew around. Here, for the first time in her life, was the father figure that had always been absent... although Rosie suspected that the new iPod, laptop, and digital camera that Andrew had recently given her might have had something to do with her mood. Ruby constantly told anyone who would listen just how brilliant Andrew was. For the first time in years, Rosie felt really alive. It was wonderful having someone who genuinely cared for her, romantically. In fact, Andrew was fitting into her and Ruby's lives so easily, that they were quickly becoming inseparable. She even quickly caught herself wondered how she had managed without him.

They would text each other every day to arrange whose house they would go to that evening – 'yours or mine', which within a week had become just 'Y or M?' More often than not, they would choose Rosie's little home. Andrew got on with Aunt Madge well, too, often collecting her and Dibble, and taking them to the dog groomers. When it fitted in with his schedule he would even drive Ruby to and from school, something that seemed to make her deliriously happy.

Before long, Andrew had asked Rosie and Ruby to move into his home, a breathtaking four-bedroom house in Westbourne Grove, not far from Notting Hill. Rosie was thrilled. It *was* a big step, she knew that, but it seemed like the most natural thing in the world to do – the next step in building their life together. Besides, Ruby's school was just around the corner from Notting Hill, and Aunt Madge was still only a short drive away. So she made arrangements with an estate agent to try and rent her own house in Hewitt Way.

Rosie and Ruby could hardly believe how beautiful their new home was. It was set over four floors, and had a very modern exterior – a curtain wall of honed black granite, with steel panels and opaque glass. Once inside, Ruby ran into the kitchen. 'Mum,' she screamed, 'you've got to look at this!' It was stunning, fitted out by a famous German manufacturer that Rosie had never heard of before.

With their jaws almost dragging on the floor, they followed Andrew up the stairs, and found themselves staring out over a beautiful view of the nearby park, thanks to some frameless, floor-to-ceiling windows.

'No *way*!' said Ruby, as she was shown her new room. 'This is, like, *a billion times* bigger than my old room.' Rosie had to agree – it was pretty special. All the bedrooms were fitted out with granite or marble en-suites.

Next to the room that she would share with Andrew was his study, equipped with a bespoke glass desk and packed with every conceivable gadget – tripods, cameras, projectors, and plenty of expensive-looking items that were a mystery to both Rosie and Ruby. You name it, he had it.

Andrew put his arms around Rosie and insisted that now it was *their* home, and that they should treat it as such. The only place, he told them, that he insisted be kept private and strictly out-of-bounds was his study. He was adamant that he should have his own personal space – 'a retreat'. After all, he reminded Rosie, he did have a business to run.

He then showed them the two outside terraces – one

on the first floor and another on the second. After he had explained how to work the music system – that ran throughout the house – and had shown them the home cinema in the basement, Ruby asked, 'Aren't you worried about getting robbed?' In a rather nonchalant way, but not bragging, he told them about the state-of-the-art security system that had been installed to keep the house and the two-car garage secure.

Rosie was lost for words. It was, without a doubt, the most beautiful house she had ever been in. True, she'd seen some gangsters' mansions back in the days with Johnny, but they seemed gaudy and fake in comparison. The only thing absent in their new home, she felt, was a woman's touch. She had been initially unwilling to bring this matter up in conversation, but when she finally did, Andrew agreed completely. So Rosie – sometimes accompanied by Andrew and Ruby, sometimes alone – went on numerous shopping trips all over London, picking out bedding, furniture and knick-knacks. Before long, the house began to look like a real family home.

Soon after moving in, Ruby had started to show interest in all things media related. When she wasn't on her new laptop – she could access the internet from her room, and spent hours chatting to her friends on social networking sites – she would be out and about playing with the new camera that Andrew had given her. It fact, she had developed a real interest in photography, perhaps inspired by Andrew, as it was one of his great passions. For Rosie, it was heart-warming to know that the two of them had a common interest and were getting to know each other.

In fact they were getting on so well that one Saturday afternoon, as Rosie was taking Ruby shopping, she looked up at her mum and said, 'Andrew's lovely, isn't he? I'm so glad that he wanted me to move in with him, as well as you.'

'Of course he did,' Rosie said. 'You wouldn't catch me moving anywhere without you.'

'He's so sophisticated… completely different from Dad,' she said. 'In fact, I wish he *was* my dad.'

Rosie stopped in her tracks, and gave her daughter an enormous hug. She could feel herself welling up. 'At least things are working out for us now, darling. Aren't they?'

'Yeah.'

'He *is* completely different from Dad, isn't he? Thank God. Well, maybe he *will* be your dad from now on. We can be a real family, just the three of us. Just as you've always wanted.'

They walked along in silence, past a long row of large display windows, before Ruby grabbed Rosie's arm and pulled her into a shoe shop.

'Mum,' she said, with a trace of fear in her voice, 'what if Sophie and the girls want to come back? Will we have to leave?'

'That won't happen, Rube. I promise. Andrew wouldn't allow that to happen… he's not like that. He's dependable, trustworthy… decent. Now, come on – what do you think of these?' she asked, picking up some bright orange trainers.

'Urgh!' Ruby exclaimed, sticking out her tongue.

Three weeks after the move, the letting agent still hadn't found a tenant for their old house, so Rosie decided to take it off their list. This was partly due to the fact that it wouldn't really bring in much money, but also because she really wasn't ready to tell Johnny that she had moved... that would open a can of worms that she really wanted to keep shut.

Whenever she went back to the old house, the answerphone would be full of messages from Johnny, and there would always be at least one letter with the familiar 'HMP Maidstone' stamp. The messages he left, for the most part, were no longer menacing. Rosie could only assume that he was involved in some new scam. The only time Johnny was ever happy was when something was going down. Whatever the reason, Rosie really didn't care, just so long as he left her alone.

Eddie, on the other hand, was proving more difficult to shake. As soon as he realised that Rosie wasn't answering the phone at home, he was constantly sending her messages on her mobile. Most of the texts concerned 'the job' he had told her about at the hotel. He was just relentless, always trying to convince her that she 'had to do it', and that she 'owed him, big time'. Her initial way of dealing with Eddie – sticking her head in the sand and not answering his calls – clearly wasn't working.

Rosie just wanted them out of her life... removed like gallstones, or a tumour. But she'd known Johnny long enough to know that that was never going to happen. He was such a possessive man that, even with him being locked away, he could still cast an imposing shadow on her new life.

Of course, Johnny was going to find out eventually… that couldn't be avoided. But Rosie was desperate to put it off as long as possible. After all, none of Johnny's friends moved in the same circles as Andrew… they would never go to the theatre or the opera – it just wasn't their bag. She did her best to forget, but every night, when Rosie's head hit the pillow, she would think of him. Johnny would go crazy if he discovered that another man was trifling with his wife. In his world, trifling with another man's wife while he's locked up is the *ultimate* taboo. Worse still, if the husband doesn't take violent retribution, then it's considered a weakness on his part. Andrew's life could be in danger.

But, despite the guilt that Rosie felt about keeping it from him, if Andrew ever mentioned Johnny she always changed the subject. She portrayed that part of her life as well-and-truly over, like it was some cesspit that she had pulled herself out of, and never wanted to revisit. Aunt Madge – the quiet voice of reason throughout Rosie's life – had told her to get it all out in the open. 'Johnny won't like it,' she said, 'but the longer you leave it, the worse it'll be. There'll be hell to pay if he hears it from Eddie, mark my words.'

But how could she tell Andrew, and risk ruining everything? He didn't have the first clue just how dangerous the twins and their friends were. Dismissing them as mindless thugs, he'd told Rosie that if they came back into her life, he'd deal with it his way… the proper way. Rosie knew that meant 'the police'… *like they could help.*

No, Rosie decided, Andrew didn't understand Johnny and Eddie, or how dangerous they could be. How could he?

nineteen

Johnny was flying high. Business was booming – three more shipments of wooden doors had arrived from Panama and, in the arches under London Bridge, the cocaine had been successfully extracted. Johnny's share was stacking up, and Eddie had recently told him that already there was £290,000 waiting for him in a safe deposit box. So, as long as the deliveries kept coming, Johnny was going a have quite a nice little nest-egg when his sentence was complete.

The Regent's Safe Depository on the Finchley Road was a favourite of London's underworld. Unlike banks, business was always conducted with no questions asked. Customers could, at short notice, access the safe depository seven days a week, 365 days a year. The beauty of the Regent's was that identity could be verified electronically, without ID. Indeed, the identity of those who used Regent's was closely guarded. Once an account was established, you need never disclose the contents of your box to anyone, so it was tucked safely away from the prying eyes of your rivals, and nosey policemen from the Financial Investigation Unit (FIU). Accessing boxes was, of course, conducted in complete privacy, inside secure viewing rooms. If you had the money, Regent's would tailor your contract to suit your requirements. In short, it was perfect for storing 'secret', unaccountable funds.

So – after every shipment had been processed, cut, and sold – Eddie would make the slow journey to the Regent's Safe Depository. Finchley Road is one of the busiest thoroughfares in London, frequently jammed with slow-moving lanes of traffic heading out of the nation's capital. Cars and vans would crawl past Lord's Cricket Ground and the multi-million pound houses of some of the country's richest hedge-fund managers, all the way to the M1.

Eddie was a regular client, and on his most recent visit, he confidently walked past the security guards, and gave a knowing wink to the pretty receptionist. She pressed the button to open the secure doors that led to the strong rooms, the secure home to 6,717 safety deposit boxes. Eddie swung his metal briefcase, which contained Johnny's latest cut, onto the table, and made his way along the rows of boxes until he reached number 743. After turning a small, brass key in the lock and sliding the box out, he returned to the table and opened it.

It contained three bundles of neatly-packed bank notes, two forged passports, some rounds of ammunition in a sealed plastic bag, and two handguns – a semi-automatic

Glock 9mm and a converted Brocock, both weapons of choice for British gangsters.

Eddie opened his briefcase and gently placed the thick stack of fifty-pound notes along side the others in the box. After four successful shipments Johnny's share was growing fast. He eyed the money greedily, his mind quickly calculating what it could buy. This wasn't the first time that he'd done this, but when it came to Johnny's cut, Eddie never missed a beat. They shared the same blood – Johnny was his twin, his shadow. Whatever the brothers did, they did it together. That's how it had always been, since they were boys. Everything was split 50-50, straight down the middle. Eddie closed the lid of the box, smiling to himself as he replaced it in slot 743.

Johnny walked with an air of confidence on C Wing – chest puffed out, head held high, and with a knowing smirk on his face. The news from Eddie had given him a real lift, not far off the feeling he used to get after a few fat lines of coke. Everything suddenly looked better, cleaner, brighter… it was all coming together. No longer did he spend the lonely hours before he could get to sleep thinking of mowing the lawn or enjoying a Sunday afternoon barbecue with the family. Now, in his head, he would visit the Regent's, open his safe deposit box, and count and re-count his cut.

Including the money from the Panama deals, Johnny now had over a million pounds stashed away… and it was still growing. When Eddie, on his last visit, asked how he was going to spend it, he'd used that old line: 'Fast cars, women, drink, drugs... I'll probably squander the rest.' He was only half joking.

The other inmates at Maidstone were happy, too. The change in Johnny was obvious and they no longer felt anxious when they spoke to him. There was no need to tip-toe around him anymore – he wouldn't blow up, like he used to. A few even felt confident enough to comment that they'd seen his wife on the TV.

In fact, Johnny found it quite funny that his wife was now a big star. When they lived together, he'd considered Rosie's earnings as her pin money. And as for her poncey acting mates, they were just mugs. He'd not for one moment considered that it would go anywhere. Even now, he still thought it was all just a flash in the pan. Besides, he and Eddie had far more important things bubbling, than concern him self with such meaningless girly trivia.

That was not an opinion that Andrew seemed to share. With the post-production on *My Fair Lady* almost complete, he was always telling her that she was destined to become a household name.

He arranged a lavish dinner party at their home to introduce her to some of his oldest friends, and had proudly announced that she 'possessed a voice that is so deep, dark and commanding that she can make a shopping list sound like erotic poetry'. Rosie had been suitably embarrassed and gave his leg a gentle kick under the table.

Andrew's friends were won over by Rosie before they had even finished their starters. One even commented that, after five minutes of listening to her talking about the joys of acting, it was easy to understand why Andrew was so completely and utterly smitten. In the flickering candlelight, wearing a daring, slinky green satin dress, Rosie looked radiant. As she glanced around the table, she felt happy to be alive.

Ruby sat beside Andrew, hanging on his every word. Earlier, when she had come downstairs in her new red dress and he had told her how lovely she looked, Ruby had felt her tummy flip over. She didn't understand why she had that reaction, or why his compliment had meant so much, but it just felt *right* that Andrew had taken the time to say that she looked nice. Her dad – *her old dad* – would never have been able to make her feel like that. Ruby was such a confident and creative girl she had slipped into her new life like slipping a hand into a well-fitting glove. She looked across at him, laughing at her mum's Eliza Dolittle accent.

'Mum, Mum,' Ruby squealed, running into the kitchen as Rosie was making after-dinner coffee for everyone. 'Guess what!'

'I don't know, Rube,' said Rosie absentmindedly, turning on the percolator, trying to remember where the 'best' cups were.

'I'm going to be a model! I'm going to be a model, just like you.'

'I'm an actress, not a model, sweetie.'

'Model, actress, what*ever*,' Ruby said. 'Andrew said he's going to help me. He *knows* people, you see. I'm going to have my photographs taken... and we're going to put a portfolio together... and then I'm going to go on "go-sees".'

'That's great,' Rosie said, rummaging in the cupboard under the sink.

'Do you even understand what "go-sees" are?'

'Hmm,' said Rosie, standing up, putting her hands on her hips, and pulling a face. 'Let me see. Are "go-sees" when you *go* and *see* an agent, by any chance?'

'Yeah, yeah, got it in one,' said Ruby, dismissively. '*Any*way, Andrew is going to help me, with all his contacts in the modelling industry. He's going to sort *everything* out, and I'm going to have professional photographs taken, and we're going to put a fabulous, fabulous portfolio together, and I will become Britain's next top model – the new, younger, and even-better Kate Moss.'

'If it's all right with your mum,' said Andrew as he entered, carrying a stack of dirty plates.

'Of course it is,' said Rosie. 'Where are the good cups? Or are you happy for them to share coffee out of Ruby's *High School Musical* mug?'

'The cupboard over the dishwasher,' said Andrew, smiling.

'Can I go on my laptop?' asked Ruby, as she poured herself a large glass of orange juice.

'Ask Andrew. You don't want to be rude to all of his friends.'

''Course you can,' he said, ruffling Ruby's hair. 'But come down and say goodbye later, okay?'

'Okay,' said Ruby, closing the fridge door.

'Who are you talking to on that computer, anyway?' asked Rosie. 'You're always online.'

'Just friends! Now, can I please –'

'Listen to me, young lady,' Rosie said, cutting her off. 'Be careful – you never know who you are talking to.'

Ruby shook her head in disbelief. 'Oh, *Mum*! Please give me *some* credit! I'm not stupid, you know. You should encourage me, like Andrew does.'

Rosie looked into dear little Ruby's eyes and smiled. She was growing up pretty quick, but was still young and innocent… and vulnerable.

'Mummy's only looking out for you, darling.'

'So I can go now?'

Rosie frowned. 'Go on then,' she said. 'But don't stay on too long. Read a book for a change!' Ruby dashed out of the kitchen and up the stairs. 'And don't forget to come and say goodbye!'

Rosie's mobile rang, and Andrew headed for the door.

'Let me know if you need help with the coffee.'

'All right,' she said, picking up her phone. She didn't recognise the number.

'Rosie Mullins,' she said. *Please don't let it be –*

'Rosie? Eddie.'

Shit! 'Look, Eddie, it's not a good time, can you call back?'

'It's on.'

'What is?'

'That favour you owe me. I'm counting on you.'

'I don't owe you any favours, Eddie!' Rosie snapped, but immediately lowered her voice, as she remembered the guests in the other room. 'I've told you a hundred times, I'm not going to do it. I'm not in *your* world any more, you know that.'

There was a long pause before Eddie spoke again. 'Johnny's been ringing you, why've you not been at home? He called every night last week… *every night*. He wants to talk to you.'

'That's not my problem.'

'You're his wife. You remember that? Or are now too big a star? You haven't got time for your family no more?'

'I've just been busy, that's all,' said Rosie, exasperated. 'Johnny and I are separated now, you know that. So I don't have to answer his calls, and I don't have to do any dirty little favours for you either. So stop ringing me, all right? Stop pestering me, or I'll…'

'Or you'll do what, Rosie Mullins?'

'Nothing. Just leave me alone,' Rosie hissed, and tuned the phone off.

She took a deep breath, filled up the coffee pot and milk jug, picked up the tray, and went through to where her guests were waiting.

'So,' she said, 'who's for coffee?'

twenty

The following Friday, Andrew had agreed to treat Ruby and a couple of her friends to a cinema trip and dinner at Pizza Hut.

'Oh God, that's brave of him,' said Stevie. Rosie, making the most of having the house to herself, had decided to make a long-overdue call to her best friend.

'You should've seen the girls getting ready earlier, all done up to the nines. Their skirts were so short, they looked more like belts! How Andrew puts up with all the giggling and squealing, I'll never know. He's a bleedin' saint if you ask me!'

'I imagine he misses having a family around; I expect he loves it,' said Stevie. 'So you weren't tempted to go with them?'

'You must be joking! I can't remember the last time I had a quiet night to myself.'

Sure enough, later that night, driving back from the restaurant, Andrew's car was full of screaming girls singing along to Beyoncé's 'Single Ladies', which was blaring from the CD player. Andrew laughed, joining in with chorus, and tapping along to the beat with his fingers on the steering wheel.

Eventually, they pulled up outside a posh mews in Chelsea, and Lucy, the last of Ruby's friends to be dropped off, got out and said goodbye. Now alone in the stationary car, Andrew turned down the music and asked, 'Had a good time, Ruby?'

Ruby nodded and continued humming along to the music.

'You are such a pretty girl... so photogenic. I can see you going a long way in modelling. I'll make sure it happens for you, I promise.' Andrew placed a hand gently on Ruby's bare knee and smiled. Ruby stopped humming.

Ruby stared up at Andrew and, due to a mixture of shock and embarrassment, found she couldn't break eye contact. Andrew's eyes were as dark as night, and were full of something that Ruby couldn't understand. He leaned over and pressed his pursed lips to hers.

Before Ruby could say a word or gather her thoughts, he had started the car, turned up the music, and they were driving through the quiet streets again, heading for home. Andrew was chatting and singing along as if nothing had happened. Ruby stared straight ahead, confused. Had she just imagined that? Or had she just been kissed? By a man. A man... and Mum's boyfriend. Had she got it wrong… read too much into it? After all, it was just a kiss. But on the lips?

All the way home, Ruby did her best to banish the thought to the back of her mind, deciding that it – 'the kiss' – wasn't meant to be anything other than a friendly gesture by a loving father-figure.

twenty-one

During the editing of *My Fair Lady*, it had emerged that the cast would have to overdub some of their scenes, so Rosie was called to spend two more days in Bristol.

Although she didn't like the idea of leaving Ruby overnight, it was the perfect opportunity to get to know Andrew's 40-acre farm in Chew Valley, which was less than half-an-hour's drive from the studio.

Brook Farm was Andrew's rural idyll – his retreat from the hustle and bustle of London, and 'a cherished slice of sanity', as he so eloquently put it – and had been in his family for five generations. He had told Rosie all about it, and she was longing to see it for herself. It was, he had explained, a former cider farm, originally dating from the 16th Century. It had a tree-lined driveway, bread oven, and even a priest's hole.

Andrew insisted that she stayed there, and gave Rosie an ancient front-door key that was so enormous it wouldn't fit into any pocket or bag.

'At least I won't lose it!' she'd said.

He suggested that she took Aunt Madge and Dibble with her, to make the most of her time away from London. 'It's completely doggie friendly,' he insisted. 'Dibble will be able to run free, no lead needed.'

'Ha! I don't know about that,' laughed Rosie, 'Aunt Madge is very protective of her precious Dibble.'

'That's in London. Wait until they get out into the countryside – it's decent, clean, and safe.'

When Rosie had asked Aunt Madge to accompany her to the farm, she'd replied with a flat 'no'. But, on reflection, and Rosie insisting that the country air would do her good and how the trip might broaden her horizons – not that Aunt Madge considered that her horizons needed broadening – she reluctantly agreed.

'But what about Ruby?' she asked. 'Ruby always stays with me when you're away. Who's going to look after her?'

'It's all taken care of. Andrew's not busy at the moment and he's got plenty of time to keep an eye on her. It's sweet, actually, he's organised a hairdresser, make-up artists and lighting engineers to come to the house for a photo shoot. Our little Ruby-two-shoes is going to be Britain's next top model. The new Kate Moss, apparently.'

Aunt Madge laughed. 'Don't *you* start! She hasn't stopped talking about it for weeks… I don't know, rabbiting on and on about Kate Moss and Heidi Plum.'

Rosie smiled. Aunt Madge was always getting her words in a twist. Once, when she was going on holiday abroad for the first time in her life, she had proudly announced that she was 'off to Dormobile'. Better known as Benidorm.

'All right, Rosie dear. Me and Dibble will come and keep you company. But,' she added, 'I want you to promise that I can collect my lottery tickets on the way, and be back Saturday in time for my programme.'

'I promise.'

Aunt Madge was a stickler for routine. The two things in her life that shared pole position in her list of priorities were Dibble and *Strictly Come Dancing* – normally just referred to as 'my programme'. Every Saturday night it was the same routine: homemade shepherd's pie followed by a slice of Walls Viennetta for tea, then she would settle down for an hour of sequined frocks and foxtrot. She especially loved watching Len Goodman, one of the show's judges. He was the virile new kid on the block, and was so popular that, Rosie suspected, he was even ranked higher than her old favourite, Brucie, who Madge had been a fan of since he hosted *The Generation Game*. The highlight of Aunt Madge's Saturday night was when Len scored 'seven'.

'Aunt Madge!' Rosie exclaimed, when she came to pick her up and saw the three bulging cases that she had packed. 'We're not going to the Outer Hebrides! It's just outside Bristol – quite civilised, you know. Plenty of culture and history.'

'Culture and history, my arse,' she said, hauling the first

case into the back of the black Range Rover that Andrew had lent them. 'Where I come from "outside Bristol" means you've got one of your boobs hanging out.'

They both roared with laughter.

'You're incorrigible,' said Rosie, helping her with her luggage. 'You can take the girl out of the East End, but you will never take the East End out of the girl.'

Before long, Rosie, Aunt Madge and Dibble were speeding along the M4 heading towards Bristol.

'You comfortable?' Rosie asked, glancing over her shoulder at Aunt Madge, who was perched in the back with her beloved dog on her lap.

'Don't you worry about us. Keep your eyes on the road, will you? We don't want to crash his lordship's new motor, now, do we? And don't forget to stop at the next service station so Dibble can stretch her legs and have a wee. I need to get my lottery tickets, too.'

Rosie looked at her in the rear view mirror. Aunt Madge had such a warm, kind face – its feathered lines were her souvenir from a long, hard life. They really didn't make them like her any more, Rosie thought. She came from a different era, when women were made of steel and grit. Dibble caught Rosie looking and gave a little growl. God, thought Rosie, she *adores* that crazy dog. She knew that Aunt Madge had even opened a savings account at the bank, so her beloved pet would be cared for in the event of anything happening. Rosie suspected that Dibble was the one thing keeping Aunt Madge alive, her reason for getting up in the morning.

They stopped at the next service station, where Dibble did her business and Aunt Madge bought her lottery tickets. Inside, near the Burger King, Rosie noticed a man who could well have been 'Harris' – the suspected policeman that had been following her – but he ducked out of sight before she could get a good look at him. As they prepared to leave Rosie looked around, trying to spot his car, but there was no sign of him. If it was 'Harris', then he was being a lot more cautious since their encounter on the train to Bristol. Rosie started the engine and, as they drove down the slip road back to the motorway, the sat-nav announced, '*Turn left.*'

'Honestly,' said Aunt Madge, shaking her head, 'where does she think we're going to go? Still, it's bloody clever. The things they can do nowadays. Who'd have thought a posh woman would be telling you where to go!'

'*Continue straight ahead,*' came the voice again, once Rosie had turned back into the middle lane.

Madge shook her head again. 'How does she know where we are?'

'Not long now,' said Rosie, smiling to herself.

As they drove, Rosie thought back to earlier in the day when she left Andrew and Ruby at the house. Ruby was trying so hard to be all grown-up. Although she was nearly 13, she really thought that she was an adult. Still, thought Rosie, this was a good step for her – it was the first time she'd been left with anyone other than Aunt Madge. Anyway, after raising his two step-daughters, Andrew would know exactly how to cope with a giggling teenager with mood swings.

When she had said goodbye, Ruby had actually physically pushed her mum away when she had gone to hug her.

'Just go, Mum. I'm not a baby.'

'Don't worry,' Andrew had said, 'she'll be fine. After her special shoot, we're having pizza, and Lucy is staying for a sleepover. So don't worry.'

She wasn't. Andrew was so good with Ruby, and she loved him to pieces. Thinking about it, Rosie remembered that she hardly ever spoke about her Johnny any more. These days it was always 'Andrew this' and 'Andrew that'. Rosie could understand why. The fathers of Ruby's school friends were all top lawyers, or high-flyers in some kind of international business. With Andrew in her life, Ruby could avoid those awkward conversations about her dad who was doing 18 years in prison for drug dealing. Her family life now fitted the respectable model that was expected by her private school.

'*Turn left at the next junction,*' ordered the sat-nav.

'There she goes again!' Aunt Madge squealed.

'Finally!' said Rosie as they turned into Brook Farm, relieved that she wouldn't have to listen to Aunt Madge's thoughts on the sat-nav for a while... until the drive home, anyway.

They drove up the half-mile, tree-lined gravel drive, and eventually arrived at the house. Parking the car by the border of the large front lawn, they got out and shook off the stiffness of the drive.

''Ave a look at that!' Aunt Madge gasped, taking in the

pretty, raised-brick borders, mature trees, and York-stone terraces with steps up to the heavy, medieval front door. 'I've never seen anything like it.'

Rosie had to agree. It was really something.

'Are you sure she can't get out?' Aunt Madge said, watching Dibble scurrying over the lawn towards some ducks.

'Andrew said it's completely doggie-proof.'

Aunt Madge set out after Dibble and caught her just as she was threatening to leap into a pond after the ducks. As she made her way back to the car, holding Dibble tight, she noticed a timber-framed potting shed and greenhouse, sheltered by a high flint wall adorned with grapevines and ivy.

As Rosie took her bag, green wellies, and new Barbour jacket from the boot, a radiant smile spread across her face. For the past year or two Rosie had been finding life in London more and more difficult. She had frequent headaches and, in recent months, had also discovered the flipside of being famous. She'd be 'spotted' numerous times while on the street and, worst of all, she had even been trailed by a member of the paparazzi for a few days. She had realised a very primal human instinct – they she didn't like being preyed upon. Andrew had been right: a few days in the country was just what she needed.

Back in London, the house was a hive of activity. Ruby's hair was tightly curled in heated rollers, while a pretty girl with a stud in her tongue applied translucent make-up.

Hanging on a rail in Ruby's bedroom were the clothes for the photo shoot – there were over 20 costumes for her to choose from. Ruby positively sparkled as she chatted non-stop with the make-up artist.

As usual, Andrew took control, moving lights and tripods into various positions, setting up shots all around the house. Ruby was too excited to even be nervous, and couldn't wait to get started. With the help of a costume dresser, she slid into her first outfit – a sparkling long gown.

For the first set of pictures, Ruby lay on a chaise longue. Andrew gently moved her arms into position and talked her through the shot.

'Treat the camera like an old friend,' he told her. 'Okay, now... relax... relax...'

Ruby smiled, and the camera clicked.

After a few more costume changes, Ruby was really settling into it. It was only towards the end of the shoot, when she changed into a bikini, that she felt suddenly uncomfortable. Looking at herself in the bathroom mirror, she felt awkward at the prospect of exposing herself in front of so many people. The costume dresser was very sympathetic and told her not to worry, offering her an alternative costume – a less-revealing beach-wear outfit with a cropped top. But it still didn't feel right.

The lighting engineers, hairdresser, and make-up girl were booked for the day and, as time was running out, Andrew went up and knocked on Ruby's bedroom door.

'Are you going to be much longer, love? We're all waiting for you.'

The costume dresser popped her head around the half-open door and shook her head.

'Poor little love,' she whispered, 'she's gone all shy. She doesn't want to do the bikini shot. It think it might be best to leave it.'

Andrew nodded and said, in a raised voice, 'Don't worry, Rube. It's okay. Let's leave the swimwear. We can always do that shot another time, okay?'

Ruby knew that he would understand – he always did.

Back downstairs, once the crew had packed up and left, Andrew turned to Ruby and said, 'You were fantastic! The pictures will be fabulous, and you'll become Britain's next top model.' He fished his mobile out of his pocket. 'Pizza time. What do you fancy? Pepperoni or just cheese and tomato?'

Ruby smiled. 'I don't mind, you choose.'

After phoning and ordering a large pepperoni and a side order of garlic bread, Andrew said, 'I didn't order anything for Lucy! When's she getting here?'

'Oh, she can't come. Her dad's back at home – he was away in New York – and he's taking her out. They're divorced. Her mum and dad.'

'Right. Oh well, it's just us two, then.'

'I'm going to pop upstairs and have a bath,' said Ruby, 'wash off the make-up, and get changed. Will you call me when the pizza arrives?'

'Of course,' said Andrew. 'No problem.'

Forty-five minutes later the pizza delivery man arrived. After paying and quietly closing the door behind him, Andrew went through to the kitchen, put the food on the table, and walked silently upstairs to Ruby's bedroom. He tapped quietly on the door and, when there was no reply, Andrew slowly turned the handle, pushed open the door and stepped inside. Ruby was in the bathroom – he could hear her splashing. For a moment, he stood perfectly still and held his breath. The only sounds he could hear were Ruby humming a tune, and the beat of his thundering heart. Then, very slowly, Andrew tip-toed towards the bathroom door. It was ajar. He stood at the door, the sweet smell of scented oils filling his nostrils. Clammy beads of sweat appeared on his top lip, and his breathing grew heavy. Peering through the crack in the door, Andrew watched as little Ruby stood up in the bath. For a moment, he drank in the sight of her nakedness. As she reached for a towel, Andrew stepped back.

'Who's that, who's there?'

Quickly shuffling back towards the bedroom door, Andrew replied, 'Pizza's here! You better hurry up, or it'll get cold.'

A little later, after tucking into their pizza in front of the television, Andrew disappeared into the kitchen. Ruby heard a loud pop, and he returned with a bottle of champagne and two glasses.

'Shall we celebrate?'

'I'm not allowed to drink!' Ruby said, giggling. 'Mum says I'm too young.'

'Well,' said Andrew, sitting down next to her, 'I won't tell her if you don't. It can be our little secret. You did so well today, I think you *deserve* a treat.' He handed her a glass. 'A toast – to Ruby, Britain's next top model.'

Ruby sipped the champagne. It tasted funny and the bubbles went straight up her nose, making her sneeze. But she didn't want to disappoint Andrew, so she gulped back the rest of the glass as if it was lemonade. Andrew watched her carefully as he refilled her champagne flute. After the third glass, Ruby was giggling and stumbling over her words. 'Thanks for today, Andrew,' she said. 'I really enjoyed it.'

'You were great. I was proud of you. It's just a shame that…'

'What?' asked Ruby, her eyes struggling to focus.

'It's a shame you couldn't do the bikini shot.'

'I'm sorry, I let you down,' said Ruby, suddenly serious. 'I just didn't want to put on the bikini in front of all those strangers. I was just shy, that's all.'

Andrew watched Ruby with unblinking eyes.

'Well, I suppose…' he said. 'Oh, maybe not'.

'No, go on. What?' asked Ruby.

'I suppose – if you want to finish off your portfolio – I suppose we could do the bikini shots now? We could do them in my study. I've got tripods, the camera, I've got everything. What do you think?'

'Um…'

'Then your portfolio would be ready to send out for agents. Without it, it's not really complete.'

Ruby thought for a moment, her head felt giddy from the champagne. 'Okay,' she said finally. 'Why not? I'm not shy in front of you.'

Andrew took a deep breath and held it. 'That's sorted then' he said. 'You pop up to your bedroom and get changed into the bikini, and I'll get set up in my study.'

He helped a rather unsteady Ruby to her feet, and she swayed across the lounge, up the stairs, and into her bedroom. She put on the bikini, her inhibitions washed away by champagne. She made her way to Andrew's study, fluffing her hair before she entered.

Opening the door, Andrew's eyes widened with excitement. Without saying a word, he took her by her tiny hand and led her to the white leather couch. He poured her another glass of champagne, which she dutifully drank within seconds.

After positioning her on the couch, Andrew stood behind the camera and started to take photos. Ruby, eager to complete her modelling portfolio, did exactly as Andrew said. After all, she told herself, he knew best… he was the expert. Finally, having taken what must have been over a hundred shots, Andrew sat on the edge of the sofa and handed Ruby a refill.

'You see? There was nothing to worry about, was there. Quite the little model now, aren't you?' He reached for her hand, and held it firmly in his. They sat that way for several minutes, until Ruby finally looked up at him.

'Can I have a smile?' Andrew asked.

In spite herself, Ruby felt her lips started to curl. She felt funny, kind of sick.

'That's better,' Andrew said. 'Now, how about a kiss?'

Ruby felt the blood rush to her cheeks. Did he mean like before? She looked at his lips, her head was swimming. She wanted him to stop talking to her, to let go of her hand.

'Perhaps you would like me to kiss you?' Andrew whispered.

Ruby's eyes dropped to the floor and she gave a breathy sort of sob. Andrew leaned forward. His lips felt warm and spongy on hers, and wet on the inside as he parted them.

'There' he said. 'Does that feel better?'

She swallowed hard, the champagne tasted horrible in her mouth. Andrew got to his feet, and slipped a hand under Ruby's hair, gently pushing her backwards across the couch. Ruby's shut her eyes tight, and felt cold as Andrew climbed on top of her. She took a deep breath, one that shook her whole body. She tried to push Andrew off, but he was too heavy. She tried to stop him, he was too strong. She tried to call out, but there were no words.

twenty-two

Rosie tried several times to contact Ruby on her mobile, but it always went straight to voicemail. Assuming that it was turned off because of the photo shoot, and not wanting to disrupt the first steps of her daughter's modelling career, she decided to try calling back later. But by ten o'clock there was still no reply to the message that she'd left, so she called the landline.

'Hi Andrew, how's it going?'

'Oh, hi! Yeah, good.'

'How's Ruby? I tried to call her on her phone, but I guess it was switched off for the photo shoot.'

'Exactly,' said Andrew, sounding as upbeat and confident as ever. 'It's lovely to hear your voice, sweetie. Well, Ruby did brilliantly… absolutely fantastic. She worked her socks off, bless her. She's a natural, a little star. In my humble opinion, she'll go a long way in this industry. And don't think that I'm saying this because she's your daughter, the truth is Ruby is very photogenic. The camera loves her nearly as much as she loves the camera.'

'Wonderful! Thank you, darling. I'm so grateful for what you've done. Can I have a quick word with her, just to say goodnight?'

'She's fast asleep. She's been so excited all day that I think it finally caught up with her. I'll get her to call in the morning.' Andrew quickly changed the subject. 'Now, please tell me, how are Aunt Madge and Dibble coping with country life?'

'She misses London, I'm afraid. She can't wait to get home... it's "her programme" tomorrow night, remember?'

'What time are you leaving?'

'I've got an early start and two short scenes, but I should be finished by lunch. Back at home by early to mid afternoon, I suppose.'

The following morning, Ruby still hadn't called. Rosie left yet another voicemail on her phone: 'Hiya, Rube. I spoke to Andrew last night. He was very pleased with you... said you're the next Kate Moss. I'll be home this afternoon. Call me back when you get this, okay? Love you.'

After listening to the message, Ruby sat on her bed staring at her mobile. Tears streamed down her face. She wanted to talk to her mum more than anything in the world, but what could she say? Her head was pounding from last's night champagne, and her private parts were burning and sore. She felt so alone – confused, frightened, and betrayed.

Hearing footsteps coming up the stairs, Ruby felt an icy wave of fear wash over her. She jumped out of bed and checked the lock on her bedroom door, double checking that it was locked. Of course it was… it had been locked since last night.

'Rube, are you up yet?' Just the sound of Andrew's voice caused her breathing to halt. She felt sick. 'I've made you breakfast, and Mummy will be home later today.'

She couldn't believe her ears. Andrew was acting as though *nothing* had happened. She stood in silence, frozen to the spot, as Andrew tried her door handle.

'Come on, love,' he said, in a sickly tone, 'time to get up.'

Ten minutes later, dressed in an old tracksuit and with her hair scraped back into a ponytail, Ruby cautiously went downstairs. Andrew was busy in the kitchen, frying bacon and singing along to the radio.

'Morning, darling,' he said. 'One egg or two?'

Ruby winced at the word 'darling'… that was what he often called her mum. 'I don't want anything,' she replied curtly.

Andrew turned off the radio, drew himself up to his full height, and turned to Ruby.

'Listen Ruby, what happened last night…' he said, quietly and affectionately. 'I won't tell your mum that you got drunk. Or that you made advances towards me. She would be so angry if she knew you betrayed her like that.'

'But… but…'

'No, Ruby,' Andrew continued, in a more commanding

191

tone, 'I think it's best if I don't tell her. I won't get you into trouble. It will be our little secret.'

Ruby didn't know what to say. She knew that she shouldn't have drunk the champagne – that would make Mum pretty mad – but what he'd done to her... well, she hadn't asked for that. She was old enough to know what had happened – she had been raped.

Looking at him, she wondered if she knew him at all. She had thought that they had a special bond – in a father and daughter way – but she had been very wrong. But what about her mum's feelings? And the house where they now lived? Ruby could feel the tears come, she was in complete turmoil. Okay, she told herself, she *had* craved for Andrew's attention. Yes, she had wanted and needed his love... but a father's love, not this.

Andrew just stared back at Ruby, watching as the tears rolled down her cheeks. This time yesterday, she never would have believed that he could be so cold and callous. He turned back to the stove, and switched the radio back on.

'So, one egg then.'

That afternoon, after dropping Aunt Madge and Dibble back home, Rosie unlocked the front door.

'Hello!' she called. 'I'm back.'

There was no reply.

'Rube, Mummy's home!'

Andrew came down the stairs, a broad smile on his face. He wrapped his arms tightly around her, kissing her on

192

the mouth and neck. She responded equally as passionately, holding him tightly.

'Mmmm... it's so nice to be back,' she said. 'So where's Ruby? My little star.'

'She's gone to Lucy's for the night. We're all alone,' he whispered.

A bolt of desire flickered through Rosie. She pressed herself against him, and found him already hard.

'I think you'd better go back and lock the front door,' she said, kissing him again. 'Just in case Ruby pops back for something.'

'Consider it done.'

By the time Andrew returned from locking the door, Rosie had removed her shirt and camisole top, and was reaching behind her to unclasp her bra. Andrew watched her undress.

'It's good to have you back,' he said, huskily.

Rosie let her hair fall loosely around her shoulders, and felt the erotic sensation of air on her bare skin. As Andrew kissed her, she gave a gasp of pleasure and slid her hand into his hair. She wanted to be naked with him, right now... his body over hers. Neither of them had any thought of time as they finished undressing, and began to make love on the floor. Tenderly at first, then even violently.

Later that afternoon, Rosie's phone buzzed, informing her that she had a text. 'Going to stay at Lucy's for weekend have taken my uniform back after school Monday x.'

193

Rosie's heart sank. She had really missed Ruby, and was disappointed not be seeing her for another couple of days. Still, she consoled herself that at least she would be able to spend some quality time alone with Andrew.

After a long, intimate weekend, Monday morning arrived along with its usual list of chores. Rosie had an audition for a feature film at two, so Andrew agreed to collect Ruby from school and pick something up for their tea.

Rosie kissed Andrew on the cheek. 'You're *so* wonderful. What would Ruby and I do without you?'

'Well, you're my girls,' he said softly. 'Aren't you? You've made me happier in the past weeks than I have been for a very long time.'

'I'm glad,' said Rosie, with a lump in her throat. 'You've done so much for us. I'm just sorry that you have deal with all of Ruby's friends… all that giggling.'

'I love it, really,' he said, smiling. 'It's all part of family life.'

Andrew parked the Range Rover as near to the school gates as possible. He was a little early, and waited patiently for the last bell of the day to ring. Eventually, the pupils started spilling out from the main gates. He watched intently, his eyes darting between their face, trying to spot Ruby. She walked out of the gate alone, looking tired. She looked across the road and, as soon as she saw Andrew's car waiting, she dropped her head and hurried away, towards the dual carriageway. Andrew leapt out of the car, as fast as a whippet, and ran over to her.

'Ruby!' he called out, as he approached. She quickened her pace but within seconds he had grabbed her arm, and spun her around. 'We need to talk.'

'I've got nothing to say to you,' she hissed, trying to wrench her arm away.

'People are staring,' he told her calmly, a thin smile fixed on his face. 'So, unless you want to cause a scene –'

'I don't care!' she screamed.

'Yes you do. Now, come along.'

Ruby reluctantly went over to his car and climbed inside, making sure that she was in the back. She didn't want to go anywhere with him… she didn't want to go back to that house. She hated it with every cell in her body, she didn't want to set foot in it again. She put on her seatbelt and stared out of the window.

'Now, listen to me,' Andrew said, as they drove along. 'Don't you think you're being selfish?'

She didn't reply.

'You're acting like a selfish, spoilt little brat. Don't you think your mother wants to see you? She's been worried. You know she's been having headaches?'

Ruby just kept looking out of the window, digging her fingernails into her palms. She wanted to scream, to tell him to leave her alone and her mum alone… but she couldn't speak. Tears were stinging her eyes. But Andrew wasn't about to stop. Wasn't what he had done bad enough?

'You're mother has sacrificed a lot for you,' he continued. 'You've always been the centre of her world, you know that.'

195

The rest of the way home, they drove in complete silence.

The moment that they arrived back, Ruby ran upstairs into her bedroom, locking the door behind her.

She didn't come downstairs for tea that evening either, no matter how many times Rosie called her.

'It's probably best to leave her,' Andrew said, as he and Rosie ate the chicken chasseur that she had prepared. 'I expect she's sulking because you went away with Aunt Madge and not her.'

'You're probably right,' said Rosie. But she was confused – Ruby had never behaved like this before. 'Teenagers, huh?'

After dinner, Rosie tapped on Ruby's bedroom door.

'Can I come in sweetie?' Trying the handle, Rosie was quite shocked to find it locked. 'Rube, open the door.'

Inside, Ruby slowly got off the bed, went over to the door, and unlocked it. Seeing the concern on her mum's face, she had a strong urge to hug her, but she fought it off and sat back down on her bed, and stared straight ahead.

Sitting beside her, Rosie looked at her daughter's face. She looked pale and troubled, and it was obvious that she'd been crying. Lifting her chin up, Rosie asked gently, 'What's up, chicken? Whatever's the matter?'

Ruby was desperate to tell her. The silence was killing her. Earlier, when she had crept out of her room and heard her mum talking with *him*, she had felt so full of guilt and self-loathing that she had even considered suicide… getting the bus to Notting Hill tube and jumping in front of a train. Looking at her mum, she knew that this pain wasn't something that a cuddle could fix… not like when she used to be afraid of the dark, or when Dad first 'went away'. Still, she did want to tell her… but how could she? Ruby was well aware of how much Andrew meant to her, she had never seen her mum this happy before. She didn't want to ruin that for her.

Rosie's heart was breaking as she watching Ruby's chin quivering. Her little eyes were full of hurt. For a few seconds the two of them sat perfectly still, not even breathing, just looking at each other in perfect silence. Ruby was, finally, on the verge of telling her everything when the moment was interrupted by footsteps on the stairs. Ruby drew back into her shell again.

'Where are my girls?' came Andrew's voice from outside.

'We're up here,' Rosie answered.

Sticking his head around the bedroom door, he said, 'Ah! Here you are. What are you two doing up here?'

Rosie felt Ruby tense up, and put a reassuring arm around her.

'We're just talking,' Rosie said.

Suddenly, Ruby jumped to her feet, and started stuffing bits and bobs into her overnight bag.

'Aunt Madge has asked me to stay with her for a couple of days. She's had one of her turns, and Dibble needs a dog walker.'

It took her under a minute to pack, and the moment she finished, she pushed past Andrew, taking care not to touch him. In a flash, she was tripping downstairs, and then Andrew and Rosie heard the front door slam.

'Phew!' Andrew sighed. 'She's in a mood.'

Despite Andrew's best efforts to reassure her, Rosie was by now really worried. It was so out of character for little Ruby… and why wasn't she talking to her? They had *always* shared their problems.

Britley House is an old, grimy, tower block in East London. Back in the Sixties, when the flats were considered modern, it was generally a safe place to live. But the years had taken their toll and nowadays the building, with its dimly-lit stairwells and walls covered with graffiti, had an uncomfortable, even dangerous, feel about it.

Aunt Madge had lived there, in a first floor flat, throughout her married life and beyond, deciding to stay on even after Uncle Bill died. 'The only way I'll ever leave this place,' she always said, 'is in a box.'

On the surface, it seemed like an unsafe place for Aunt Madge and Dibble to stay, but none of the youths who loitered around at night like feral dogs would dare say one word out of place to her or anyone visiting her. She had, through Rosie, a link to the name of Mullins, and everyone in the East End knew better than to disrespect that. So that night, when Ruby made her way up the stairwell, past the noisy teenagers drinking cheap cider and smoking joints, they all stepped silently out of her way.

Aunt Madge welcomed her inside – her flat felt warm, cosy, safe. After making them a cup of tea, Aunt Madge sat down in her well-worn armchair and put her feet up on the pouffe. Dibble took her place in front of the gas fire, with one bar blazing orange. Ruby sat on the other chair, quiet. Aunt Madge eventually broke the silence.

'What's up, Rube?'

Ruby shook her head, unable to answer.

'Is it school? Are you being bullied?' she asked.

'It's nothing,' Ruby mumbled, 'I'm just tired. I think I'll go to bed now.'

'Aren't you going to finish your tea?'

'I don't really feel like it. Good night.' Ruby got up, leaned over, and kissed her on the forehead.

'Night-night, sweetheart,' said Aunt Madge. 'Sleep tight. Don't let the bed bugs bite.'

Ruby lay down on her bed and started crying. She cuddled her pink teddy, Mimim, and pushed her face into the duvet to muffle the sobs. She just wished she could go back to how it was a week ago. But she wasn't crying just because of what happened, Ruby was also scared about what *would* happen. Andrew seemed capable of anything... would he do it again? He might even *kill* her, she thought. But then, at least, he wouldn't be able to do things to her any more and this horrible feeling would go away.

She had been prepared to tell Aunt Madge everything, but she hadn't been able to find the words. Who did she know that she could tell *anything*? Who would believe her?

In a locker in a gym in Florida, a mobile rang. It wasn't until an hour later, when Stevie had finished her aerobics class, that she picked up the message. What she heard stopped her in her tracks – it was the sound of someone sobbing down the line. She couldn't make out any words apart from her own name, but the crying sounded like someone's heart was breaking. She pressing a key, and played the message back again. After looking at the call log, her suspicions were confirmed… it was Ruby.

'Rube, darling? It's Auntie Stevie,' she said, when Ruby answered. 'I didn't wake you did I?'

'No.'

'Are you okay? I just got your message. What's wrong sweetheart?'

'Nothing, I'm okay.' She still sounded close to tears. 'Aunt Stevie, when are you coming home? When are you coming back to London? I miss you?'

'Not for a while, sweetie,' Stevie said. 'What's wrong? Is it Dad?'

'No, no… it's okay. Everything's cool. Sorry I called, but –'

'I'm *always* happy to hear from you, Rube. Don't apologise.'

'I have to ring off now, Auntie Stevie.'

The line went dead. Stevie immediately selected 'Rosie' from her list of contacts, and pressed 'call'. Rosie answered on the second ring.

'Rosie? Great, you're there,' she said. 'I thought you might be on set.'

'No, we're finished shooting,' Rosie said. 'So what's up?'

'Well,' said Stevie, hesitantly, 'I'm not sure. Ruby left me a message earlier. I couldn't make out what she was saying, she was sobbing so hard. I rang her back but she said she was cool. Is she at home?'

'No, she's at Aunt Madge's,' Rosie said, with a sigh. 'Something's going on with her. But she won't tell me anything. She's been acting really weird lately. I don't know… maybe it's school… too much homework or maybe the school. Could it be a boy? Whatever it is, she won't eat with us – she's locking herself in her room. I just don't know what's wrong.'

'That doesn't sound like her at all.'

'No. To be honest, I'm losing patience with her. I don't want to sound unsympathetic – I'm not – but I can't imagine what she's got to complain or be upset about.'

'Poor little lamb, she's obviously having a tough time of it lately. Someone needs to spoil her a bit… and if a Godmother can't do that, then I don't know who can. I'll take her shopping next time I'm over. Look after her. I have to go. Give my love to Andrew.'

After she rang off, Rosie was puzzled. Why on earth would Ruby ring Stevie in America? What was going on with her? She had to get to the bottom of this.

The next morning, after breakfast with Aunt Madge, Ruby switched on her mobile phone and punched in a six-digit number.

'Oh, yes,' she said, as her call was answered. 'Can you get me the number for… Mullins Business, I think it is. It's in Limehouse.'

'I've got a "Mullin's Export",' said the voice after a few seconds. 'Shall I put you through?'

'That's it,' said Ruby. 'Yeah, put me through please.'

As the phone rang, Ruby wondered if this *really was* the right thing to do.

'Hello, Mullins Exports. Sharon speaking, can I help you?' came the chirpy voice.

'Yes, erm, can I speak to Mr Mullins please. Eddie,' Ruby asked.

'Who's calling, please?' asked Sharon, sounding a mixture of surprised and bemused.

'It's… it's his niece, Ruby.'

'Oh, right. Well I'm sure Uncle Eddie would love to talk to you. Hang on and I'll put you straight through.'

While waiting, Ruby's face grew pale. Her hand was clenched so tightly around the phone that her knuckles were perfectly white.

Finally, Eddie's voice came thundering down the line. 'Ruby! Well, there's a turn-up for the books! How are you, chicken? What can I do for you?'

Ruby took a breath. 'I was wondering…'

'What? Spit it out.'

'I… er… I… Can I see my dad? Can you arrange it, Uncle Eddie? Can you arrange for me to go see my dad in prison?'

'Of course I can, darling,' said Eddie, taken aback. 'What's wrong?'

'Nothing,' said Ruby. 'I just want to see my dad, that's all. I just miss him.'

'Well… I suppose so. Yeah, I could do that for you.'

twenty-three

Rosie was understandably upset when Ruby told her that she had phoned Uncle Eddie, and that he was taking her to visit her dad in prison. Why did she want to see him, of all people? It was especially surprising, as they had done so well in building a new family unit with Andrew. She hadn't ever really bothered with Johnny before – if anything, he'd been a bit of an embarrassment to her – so why now? But then again, Rosie was painfully aware that Ruby hadn't been herself lately, so if a visit to Johnny would help her recover, then it was worth a shot. Ruby had been adamant that Rosie didn't tell Andrew she was going – she doesn't want to hurt his feelings, Rosie thought – so she kept her word and didn't mention it.

It was around lunchtime the following Saturday when a sleek, metallic silver SL class Mercedes pulled smoothly into the car park adjacent to Britley House. The trio of teenagers who were kicking a football against a battered garage door abruptly stopped when they recognised the personalised number plate. They picked up their football, and stared with a degree of awe as the formidable-looking man climbed out of the car. Eddie needed no introduction to anyone 'in the know' in the East End. Even though he hadn't been to Britley House for a couple of years, everyone on the estate knew who exactly who he was. The brothers, as locals who had 'done good', were almost worshiped in certain circles.

Hate-'em-all was with him, but he decided to wait by the car... not to guard it – nobody would dare touch it – but rather because of Dibble. Harry hated even the most placid dogs, so whenever Dibble ever came up in conversation, he would complain that, 'If it were up to me, I'd have that fucking psycho dog put down, I would.'

Eddie strolled across the parking bays, past the walls covered with scrawled 'tags', the boarded-up doors, and the windows protected by iron bars. The corridors and stairwells were filthy, and Eddie sneered as he picked his way through the empty Coke cans, fag ends and the occasional used condom.

Although Eddie and Aunt Madge never really saw eye-to-eye, there was a degree of mutual respect, which always surprised Rosie. Eddie always watched his Ps and Qs around her, out of respect for her plucky spirit and grit, honed during the Blitz. In turn, Aunt Madge respected his 'old school ways' – not something to be taken for granted these days, she thought.

Aunt Madge's highly-glossed red door had an

immaculately polished door knocker and a doormat with two black paw prints printed on it. Eddie straightened his cuffs and adjusted his tie before ringing the bell.

'Hello, Aunt Madge,' Eddie said, as she opened the door, holding Dibble under one arm. 'How ya keepin'?'

Looking up, she replied with a simple 'Eddie', searching over his shoulder for his sidekick Hate-'em-all. She never liked him… she could never trust anyone who didn't like a dog as sweet and good-natured as her Dibble.

Ruby appeared in the doorway, clutching a small bag, and Aunt Madge gave her a beautiful smile, full of reassurance and love.

'Call if you need anything, Rube, okay?' she said. 'You've got your mobile?'

Ruby nodded. 'Hi, Uncle Eddie.'

'Hello, love,' Eddie said.

After spitting on the corner of her handkerchief and wiping a speck of dirt off Ruby's face, Aunt Madge said goodbye. Eddie led Ruby along the landing, her hand looked miniscule, grasped gently by Eddie's fat fingers. As they went down the steps, two young boys who were sitting and sharing a cigarette in the stairwell, swiftly edged out of their way.

'Good lads,' Eddie muttered, as they passed them.

By the time Ruby, Eddie and Hate-'em-all-Harry arrived at HMP Maidstone it had started to rain. Although the one-way system was as busy as ever, the only people on the street was a line of visitors, huddled under umbrellas, waiting to go inside the prison. Ruby flinched when she heard the squeaking sound of bolts being drawn back and a key being turned in a lock. The small door within the huge oak gate creaked open and the visitors began to shuffle inside.

Ruby hadn't seen her dad in prison for five years. In the early days of his sentence both Rosie and Johnny felt it better if their daughter wasn't dragged all over the country on visits. Rosie always showed her pictures of her dad, and they spoke on the phone fairly regularly, too, but still their relationship was far from conventional. Now, as Ruby waited patiently outside the prison that held him, she did begin to panic that, once inside, she wouldn't recognise him.

With surprising tenderness, Eddie led Ruby inside, where she was frisked by a burly female prison officer. She wanted to impress her uncle and Harry, so did her best to take everything in her stride, even trying not to blink when a security camera took her image.

Ruby looked, and felt, smaller than her 12 years when she was led into the vast visiting hall. She dutifully took a seat at the battered and chipped Formica-topped table, while Eddie and Harry collected tea and snacks from the canteen. After what seemed like an hour, a loud electronic buzzer sounded, making Ruby jump. A heavy iron door swung open and a short officer with a thick moustache nodded to the Control, a sign that a category 'A' man was coming through.

Johnny filled the doorway. Ruby was surprise at the size

of her dad – thanks to five years of working-out at the prison gym he had honed his stocky, British bulldog figure – but she recognised him immediately. The sight of him, in a white t-shirt and jeans, wearing a chunky Cartier bracelet on one wrist and a gold Rolex on the other, brought back a flood of memories. He had darker skin than she remembered, but the jet-black hair and cornflower-blue eyes were unmistakable. Spotting her, Johnny gave one of his rare smiles.

Ruby stood up. 'Daddy!' she cried, involuntarily spreading her arms.

Johnny rushed over and scooped her up in his arms. When she kissed him on the cheek, Johnny felt the unfamiliar sensation of a lump in his throat, and tears welling up in his eyes. It had been so long, he had almost forgotten... he had almost lost her.

'Haven't you grown up' he said, putting her down and stepping back for a better look. 'You're *beautiful*. The dead ringer of your mother.'

Father and daughter sat next to each other, her arms wrapped tightly around his massive bicep. Sitting there with him, Ruby felt something that she hadn't felt for what seemed like forever: safe... untouchable.

Eddie and Hate-'em-all returned with a tray of snacks and put it down on the table. Johnny couldn't take his gaze from his daughter. With her clear skin and pretty eyes, she looked *so* much like Rosie. Over the course of the two-hour visit, he must have used the word 'stunner' over 20 times. Ruby, on the other hand, didn't say much at all – she seemed kind of shy – she just nodded in all the right places, and smiled sweetly.

Inside, Ruby was in turmoil. She was desperate to talk to her dad about what had happened to her, but Rosie had given her strict instructions not to tell her father that they were no longer living in Hewitt Way. 'If he finds out that Mummy has a boyfriend,' she had told her, 'there will be no end of grief.'

As Johnny, Eddie and Hate-'em-all sat around talking in hushed tones about 'deliveries', Ruby tried to think of a way to tell her dad about Andrew without getting her mum into trouble. Eventually, with time running out, she spoke up.

'Dad? I...'

'What is it, Ruby?'

'Can... can I come and see you again?'

'Of course you can,' Johnny said, with a wink. 'Why don't you bring Mum next time?'

Ruby tried again. 'Dad, Dad... I want to tell you something. I want to tell you something *on your own*.'

Sensing something wrong, Johnny said his goodbyes to Eddie and Harry, who told Ruby they would meet her outside. Once they had left, Johnny turned to his daughter.

'What's up darling? Tell me,' he said. 'Whatever it is, daddy will fix it. Listen, I know I haven't always been a good dad – what with all the problems I had before – but I've always loved you. You know that, don't you? And I always will love you, too. There's *nothing* I wouldn't do for you.'

Ruby took a deep breath. A tear – *a little diamond*, Johnny remembered Rosie's name for Ruby's tears – dropped from her eye. Johnny wiped it away with his finger, and looked deep into her pretty blue eyes. There was, he could see, a bleak sadness in there.

'What's up darling? Come on, you can tell Daddy.'

twenty-four

Rosie had a surprise for Andrew. His birthday was coming up, and Rosie had been called away to Brighton for a read-through and a series of meetings about a new film. She had expected to stay in Brighton overnight, but they had finished earlier than expected, so she made a last-minute arrangement to catch a train back to London to surprise him. He was off to Thailand – to film a documentary this time – and Rosie was overjoyed that she'd be able to see him before he left. It also meant she would be able to give him the new leather briefcase and hand-made birthday card that she had bought him.

After paying the taxi driver, Rosie let herself into the house where she heard muffled voices coming from the lounge. Deciding to climb into their bed and wait for him, Rosie quietly closed the front door behind her and tip-toed up the stairs. As she passed his private study she was surprised to see that the door was ajar. Andrew's study was *always* locked. She thought it odd, but welcomed the opportunity to sneak in and put the card on his desk. He'd

210

open it and read, 'Come next door for your *real* present!' *Perfect*. She crept into the study and, finding a space on the desk next to his computer, she opened the card and began to write inside it.

At that moment she heard a 'bleep' – Andrew had an incoming email. She glanced over at it, and noticed a pile of photographs, the top one lying face down. Eager to see Ruby's portfolio pictures, Rosie turned it over. It was Ruby all right, but there was something terribly wrong. Her daughter was wearing a bikini… a rather revealing bikini. She was lying on the white leather sofa that Rosie had noticed on the way into the study. Why would he have taken her picture in here? A scantily clad 12-year-old in a man's private study. That wasn't the type of photo shoot that Rosie had agreed to at all. Picking up the next photo, her very worst fears were confirmed: it was her little Ruby, topless. Instantly, a thick blackness descended, enveloping Rosie's soul.

She couldn't breathe.

Her stomach cramped up like she was going to be sick.

With her hands shaking so much she could hardly hold the photos, she thumbed through the others. Each one was worse than the last. How could this be? Andrew went to the local church… he ran his own company… he played golf at the local country club. He was so sophisticated… so decent. What were these photos doing there? It seemed so unlikely, that Rosie struggled to understand what they meant. The photos dropped from her hands, and she stood in silence on trembling legs.

211

She only snapped out of it when the computer made another bleeping sound. Still in a daze, Rosie opened the message. To her disgust Rosie discovered that Andrew had been logged on to a chatroom, and was messaging someone with the username 'Sexy Suzy'. Reading the message Rosie was shocked: 'Hi Corky, gotta be quick mums downstairs =) attached is picture you wanted'.

Rosie clicked the mouse, opening the attachment. There in front of her was a picture of young girl lifting her top up and exposing her naked breasts. The message continued, 'will you meet me Corky? You promised you would if I sent you that pic. xxx'.

Scrolling through the filthy message, Rosie grew more and more shocked and horrified and scrolled through the other messages. Their words seemed to jump out of the screen, mocking her – 'fuck', 'bitch', 'sexy' – and all of them were signed 'Corky'. Rosie couldn't believe what she was seeing. Not her Andrew? It couldn't be.

Suddenly, she heard his voice downstairs, bidding his guests farewell. Rosie hurriedly picked up the pictures of Ruby and put them back on the desk. Then she hastily left the room, taking the birthday card. In blind panic she quietly scurried up the next flight of stairs to Ruby's bedroom on the top floor. She closed and locked the door, and sat on her daughter's bed. There, sitting in the dark, everything fell into place.

Rosie put her head in her hands and wept. She wept so hard, she had to force her face into the pillows to muffle the sound – just as Ruby had – so Andrew wouldn't know she was there. She listened as he returned to his study. As she finally drifted off into a troubled sleep, he was still there.

The sound of the front door slamming woke her the next morning. Rosie lay motionless, staring up at the ceiling, and listened to the car start and pull away. She thanked God that he had left for a 10-day trip – to shoot footage for a documentary about tigers – so she wouldn't have to face him.

Looking around the room, all Rosie could think about was Ruby, and what had happened. She quickly put on her shoes, went downstairs, and called a cab.

Aunt Madge and Ruby were watching GMTV when the doorbell rang. When Aunt Madge saw Rosie's ashen face, she knew instantly that something was terribly, terribly wrong. Rosie ran through to the lounge, knelt down by her daughter, grabbed her tightly, and burst into tears. Ruby didn't respond at first, just stayed stiffly locked in her mother's embrace. But eventually the tears came – and when they did, they lasted for a very long time.

Eventually, when their tears began to subside, Rosie took Ruby's face in her hands and, running her fingers through her hair, gently asked: 'My dear, sweet Ruby. Can you tell me now? Can you tell me what happened?'

'He's not coming here?' Ruby asked.

'No, baby. He's not coming anywhere near you.'

'I hate him,' Ruby said, hugging her mum tighter. 'I *hate*

him! I wish he was dead.' She banged her fists against her mother. 'You don't understand… he made me… *do* things, Mum. He said it's what I wanted, but I *didn't*. I *hated* it when he touched me, and when he made me touch him.'

The words hit like a steam train. A thin, painful sound came from Aunt Madge.

'He says it was *my* fault,' Ruby choked desperately, her face was ravaged with confusion. 'I want him to stop. Now.'

'Just tell me what he did to you,' Rosie said fiercely. 'I need to know. You say he touched you? Where?'

'Here,' she said, putting her hand to her chest, 'and here,' moving it to her groin.

Rosie thought she was going to faint. 'Did he… Rube, did he force himself on you?' Her daughter's eyes dropt to the floor. 'Ruby, you have to tell me. Did he?'

Ruby nodded, and burst into tears.

Getting to her feet, her eyes blazing with rage, Rosie looked over at Aunt Madge, who stood, open-mouthed and shaking. Rosie went over and hugged her. Putting her head on the arm of the chair, Ruby's sobbing reached a new pitch and, for what seemed like an age, the three of them all cried together.

Suddenly, Rosie remembered that Ruby had gone to visit her father in prison.

'Baby,' she said, kneeling down by the chair, 'did you tell Daddy what happened to you?'

Wiping the tears from her eyes and blowing her nose,

Ruby shook her head. 'I wanted to tell him, I tried to tell him – but I just couldn't.'

'Thank God, Rube. Thank God.'

Once Ruby was tucked up in bed, Rosie sat down in front of the gas fire, reached over and gripped Aunt Madge's hand. She was a wry old fox – the glue that kept the family together – and Rosie was happy that, out of all of the people she knew in the world, that she was the one with her that night. They sat up half the night discussing what had happened. Aunt Madge had told Rosie that she had a close friend in Britley House whose daughter was a doctor – she'd be able to check that Ruby would recover, physically at least.

As they talked, Rosie realised, to her great shame, that it was her desire to be 'respectable' – to change her life and get away from Johnny's world – that had clouded her judgement. Her desire for what she believed Andrew stood for led her to miss what was going on right under her nose. Perhaps this was why Andrew's first wife, Sophie, kept him away from her daughters? Perhaps he had done the same to them? Aunt Madge was convinced that was the case.

'We can't let that bastard get away with it,' Aunt Madge said. 'Whatever happens, he's not going *near* another little girl ever again.'

They discussed going to the police, but Rosie knew that her word wouldn't count for much with them, considering that she was a Mullins and that they were so suspicious of her that they already had someone following her. Also, the publicity that would surround such a sordid revelation would be too much for her and Ruby to handle. Plus, if Johnny read a story like that in the papers... God only knew what he would do. Reluctantly, at Aunt Madge's recommendation, she decided to call Eddie.

The following morning, Rosie sat in her car, looking up at an ultra-modern block of flats in Canary Wharf in London's Docklands. It was many, many years since she had been there... and, given the choice, she would never go there again.

Reaching the large, plate-glass front door of the block, she found Eddie's buzzer and gave it a short sharp blast. She glanced over her shoulder and spotted someone, loitering far behind her – it was 'Harris'. *Great, this is just what I need.* She'd been with Johnny long enough to know that this meant she was under surveillance, probably 24 hours a day. They would follow her *everywhere*. Although she knew that her visiting Eddie was exactly the kind of behaviour that the police were probably looking for, she had more important things to worry about.

Finally, the doors clicked and began sliding apart. Rosie walked into the marble lobby where a security guard was stationed behind a reception desk. He barely looked up as she passed, too engrossed in the Chelsea game that he was watching on a portable television to notice anything else. The lift rose so smoothly up to the 25th floor that Rosie hardly noticed it was moving.

When she knocked on Eddie's door, it edged open and she stepped inside. The familiar scent of aftershave hit her immediately.

'We're in here,' Eddie shouted, hearing footsteps on the marble floor.

Passing the plush bathroom and two more bedrooms, Rosie walked in to the sitting room. Standing in front of the large windows overlooking the churning brown waters of the Thames, stood Eddie and Hate-'em-all-Harry.

'Well, girl,' he said, 'what the fuck's going on?'

'Eddie...' Rosie began, as the familiar rush of tears came.

'Well? What is it?'

'It's Ruby,' she sobbed. 'She's... she's... she's been raped.'

Eddie took a sharp intake of breath.

'She's been *what*!'

twenty-five

Rosie sat, her head bowed and her highlighted auburn hair obscuring her face. She kept her gaze fixed at the floor as she explained, in a flat, monotonous voice no more than a whisper, just what had happened to Ruby.

Retelling the story, she went through the gamut of emotions, but the one she felt most sharply was guilt – guilt that she had been so blinded by her desire to escape from Johnny's world… guilt that she had not got to know Andrew better before moving in with him. *How could I have been so stupid?* Surely the clues were there? An ex-wife who wouldn't let him near her daughters… a private study that no one was ever allowed in. With hindsight – and hindsight is such a wonderful thing – the problem was very obvious.

Eddie and Hate-'em-all listened in shock as the story slowly unfolded. Compared to the news about Ruby, the revelation that she had been secretly living with Andrew – using Hewitt Way as just a mail drop – seemed just like background information. Deciding that it would be best to be completely up-front, Rosie gave them every last detail. They might not like to hear it, but they had the right to know.

When she had finished, Hate-'em-all-Harry got up and made his way to the window. Looking out over London, he started to speak. He was a man of very few words, so when he spoke, people always listened.

'I've been around the block, and then some... and got the scars to prove it. I thought I'd seen it all. But this?' The fury seemed to be seeping out of every pore in his body. 'What sort of fucking *animal*... Johnny's *daughter*.'

Rosie got up out of her seat but, as she tried to stand, her legs gave way beneath her. As she sank to the ground, Eddie caught her, wrapping his thick arms around her belly, and hauled her up.

'Who else knows about this?' he said in a hoarse whisper, so close that Rosie could feel his breath on her face.

'Aunt Madge and me.'

'Where is he? Where is this *bastard*?'

'He's in Thailand, on business.'

'Thailand?' said Eddie.

'Yeah, right. *Business*,' said Hate-'em-all, his voice thick with sarcasm.

'He's filming tigers,' Rosie said.

'Are you thick, or just plain stupid?' Eddie asked, as he dropped Rosie back onto the sofa. His eyes were boring into her. 'There aren't any tigers in Thailand! They're in... fucking India!'

Rosie looked at Eddie, then to Hate-'em-all. They could almost hear the cogs in her brain clicking into gear. The penny dropped.

'Oh my God… Thailand?' Rosie gasped. 'You mean…'

'Yes,' Eddie said, '*Thailand*.'

Throughout their brief relationship, Andrew had taken many trips to Thailand and Cambodia. He always appeared to have a valid reason to go and, besides, Rosie never had any reason to question him… why should she? As far as she was concerned, he didn't have any reason to lie. He was decent, respectable, a pillar of the community. Or, at least, that was what she had thought.

Eddie and Hate-'em-all looked at each other. They knew each other well enough to know what they were thinking – this bloke was the one thing that career criminals hated the most: a child rapist. A nonce. A pervert. To add insult to injury he had taken a liberty with a Mullins. When it came to business, if you crossed Johnny or Eddie and they found out, the retribution was terrifying. But this? This carried only one punishment, and both Eddie and Hate-'em-all knew that the punishment would neither be quick nor painless.

Rosie could guess what their silence meant.

'I'm thinking of going to the police. They come down heavy on people like him.'

'Oh yeah, is that right?' Eddie said. 'So what the fuck are you doing here, then? No, wait. Don't answer that. I'll tell you why – you don't want the newspapers to get hold of the story. It might ruin your career, is that it?'

'No!' Rosie cried. 'Of course not. What kind of person do you think I am? It's because of Ruby. I just can't put her through that. She's been through enough. I don't care about my career… it means nothing to me. *Nothing*. Don't you know me at all?'

'I'll tell you what I know,' said Eddie, his eyes narrowing. 'I know little Ruby was abused – *raped* – by a nonce. A limp, dandelion-fucking nonce, that *you* slept in the same bed with. That's what I know, Rosie!'

'Eddie, do you think for one –'

'Oi!' Hate-'em-all's thunderous voice cut the argument dead. 'Listen a minute. Rosie, when you saw those messages on his computer, did you see the email address?'

'It was a chatroom, but I remember his user name – "Corky".'

'Right,' said Eddie, picking up on the idea and turning to Hate-'em-all. 'Call Computer Terry. Tell him I want to see him. Now.'

'Ok,' said Hate-'em-all, reaching for his mobile.

'We'll catch that bastard,' Eddie said. 'I'll make sure of that.'

'What about Johnny?' Rosie asked, aware that she had set events in motion that she could no longer control.

Eddie stopped dead. 'Do you think I could tell him? *Do ya*?' he screamed.

Rosie shrunk back in her seat. 'Please! Don't bark at me.'

'I think there's only one dog in this room, Rosie. Don't you?'

221

Eddie paced like a caged animal until the buzzer sounded. Hate-'em-all got the door, and in walked a tall, skinny man in his early thirties who wore a tattered brown leather jacket and an AC/DC t-shirt. 'Computer Terry', as Johnny had christened him, was a real expert in electronics, and the only man that Eddie trusted to set up his computers.

There was no time for niceties or pleasantries – Terry just got straight down to business.

'So, who are we after?' he asked, opening his laptop on the glass-topped coffee table.

Within ten minutes he had hacked into the chatroom's records and got hold of Andrew's log-in details. Three minutes later, he was into his private email address. And within half-an-hour he had bypassed the security and was casually browsing Andrew's private files.

'Oh fucking 'ell,' exclaimed Terry, after clicking onto a file named 'TL6'.

A collection of photographs flashed onto the screen that shocked them all – they were explicit images of a very young Thai girl being horribly abused. Although the man's face was out of shot, Rosie knew without a doubt that it was Andrew.

That was just the tip of the iceberg. Terry accessed file after file, containing countless images of child pornography. Then Computer Terry uncovered a file of videos that Andrew had filmed, using a webcam, of himself 'performing'.

'All right,' said Hate-'em-all, 'we get the idea. That's enough.'

'So,' said Eddie, turning on Rosie again, 'this is your

respectable lover boy, is it? You know the one… he's out in Thailand filming tigers!'

'Fucking animal,' said Terry. 'He should be strung up.'

'Don't you worry,' growled Hate-'em-all, 'I'll take care of that, all right?'

'How are we going to get hold of him?' said Eddie.

'Well,' said Terry, 'you've got his username, email address…'

'Keep talking,' said Eddie.

'Why not use a honey trap? You could set up an email, pretend to be a young girl – a friend of this "sexy Suzy", or something – and then hang around in that chatroom until he turns up.'

'Has he taken his laptop to Thailand?' Eddie asked Rosie, now visibly shaking.

'I assume so.'

'Right, so while he's away, we start sending him emails, play along. We could even send a picture of any random little girl, just to keep him interested.'

'Yeah,' said Hate-'em-all, 'and then tell him that her parents are going away and she'd he like him to come and visit. Somewhere out of the way, you know. And we just wait for him to show up.'

'You'd have the bastard,' said Terry, 'bang to rights.'

'Blinding!' said Eddie. 'Sort it, Terry… now.' He was now thinking on his feet, running through the logistics. 'But where shall we do it?'

'It can't be the middle of nowhere,' said Terry, 'he'd cotton on.'

'But it can't be in the middle of town, either,' said Hate-'em-all. 'Too many people. We can't risk any prying neighbours who might overhear.'

'I know just the place,' said Eddie finally. 'What about that little bungalow on the edge of Epping Forest?'

'Oh yeah,' said Hate-'em-all. 'That would be perfect.'

Rosie was now feeling like a bystander. Eddie was on a roll and she knew that there was nothing anyone could do to stop him.

As she was getting ready to go back to Aunt Madge's to see Ruby, while Hate-'em-all and Terry set up a bogus user account on the chatroom, Eddie took Rosie aside.

'You get out of that house, you understand? Pack up your stuff and go back to Hewitt Way – that's where you're supposed to live. When the nonce rings, you act normal. Don't give anything away. Ruby should stay with Madge… I don't want that bastard around her ever again. You get me?'

Rosie nodded.

'He will not see her ever again… he won't even *speak* to her. If I find out he's been anywhere *near* her, Rosie, once I'm done with him, I'll come after you. Do I make myself clear?'

Rosie went cold. She knew he meant every word he said.

'Then,' Eddie continued, 'you give up your silly acting, and get back to what's expected of you. You are Rosie Mullins, Johnny's wife.'

'What are you going to tell him?'

'Nothing. I'm not going say a word about this. Not for your sake either, but for Johnny's. It would *kill* him if he knew. Anything could happen. Nah, me and Harry will take care of this.'

Terry interrupted them. 'Listen, how's this? "Hiya corky, sexy Suzy said you are cool. I'm thirteen, how old are you?" That's all right isn't it?'

'That'll do,' said Eddie. 'Send it.'

twenty-six

Rosie enlisted the help of two strong men from Aunt Madge's estate to help with the imminent move from Notting Hill back to Hewitt Way, and hired a van to carry all their belongings. That night, as she sat in Aunt Madge's little flat, with Ruby on her knee, her phone beeped. She had a four-word text from Eddie. It read: 'He replied. It's on.'

She turned off her phone and put it on the side table, next to her cup of tea.

'Rube?'

'Yeah?'

'I can promise you that no one will ever hurt you again.'

The big move couldn't happen quickly enough for Rosie or Ruby. She directed events from Andrew's house, while Ruby and Aunt Madge waited at Hewitt Way for the removals van to arrive. It was a day of mixed emotions for all of them.

There was less than a week left before Andrew was due to return from Thailand, and she wanted everything that they owned to be removed from his house by the time he came back. She knew she was never going to return there.

As Rosie packed up their things into large cardboard boxes, she was surprised to see how much she and Ruby had accumulated since they arrived. But, finally, the last box was crammed into the back of the van. Rosie took her bunch of keys and security fobs from her handbag, locked the door, and pushed them back through the letterbox. Walking away from Andrew's house, she felt a huge sense of relief. She was leaving behind the respectable life that she had once craved – she'd tried so hard to fit in with Andrew's friends – but she knew that it was nothing she'd really miss. *Funny*, she thought, *I was convinced I'd cracked it*. Goodbye to all that phoney conversation, those opera and theatre trips, the Chablis and lobster. With a bitter smile, she thought how perfect she had been for the part of Eliza Dolittle – the woman who didn't fit into either world… the woman who didn't belong anywhere.

The traffic was fairly light for a Saturday evening, so it didn't take long for the van to drive back to Hewitt Way. When Rosie opened the front door, it was like stepping back in time. The house was warm and inviting, just like it had always been.

'Oh, it's you, Mum,' Ruby said, running over and giving her a peck on the cheek.

Aunt Madge gave instructions to the helpful removal

men, and Ruby picked up one of her boxes and carried it upstairs.

'Cup of tea?' asked a familiar voice.

Rosie's eyes widened with surprise as she looked up to see Stevie coming towards her, carrying a large foil plate of freshly cut sandwiches and a mug.

'Stevie!' she said. 'What's all this?'

After a long hug, they sat down with Aunt Madge at the table. As they poured the tea and ate the sandwiches, a wonderful, safe feeling came over Rosie. It felt so good being back at her home, surrounded by the people she loved. Looking around she saw the worn, old sofa, the small coffee table, the bookcases attached to the wall, the little knick-knacks that made it home... they were all there, like they had been waiting for her.

Aunt Madge put a reassuring arm around Rosie and gave her a squeeze. 'Things will be all right, darling,' she said. 'Just you wait and see.'

Rosie nodded and gave a watery sniff. 'I really didn't know,' she said. 'I really didn't know.'

'It's okay, Rosie,' said Stevie, pulling her into an embrace.

Tears rolled down Rosie's cheeks as she looked around the room. 'It's good to be home,' she said, her voice barely making it past the knot in her throat.

Later that night, after Aunt Madge had left and while Stevie was doing the washing up, Rosie wandered around the house, re-acquainting herself with it. The small rooms and cheap, faded furniture that she had previously hated, she now looked at with fondness. Thank God, she thought, that she was still had this little island of warmth and shelter.

'You awake?' she whispered, sticking her head in to Ruby's room.

'Yeah,' came her daughter's sleepy voice.

'You okay?'

'Yeah.'

'I'm downstairs if you need anything, okay?'

'Okay.'

'Goodnight Rube,' Rosie said, closing the door.

'Mum?'

'Yeah?'

'I never want to leave here again.'

'Okay,' said Rosie, 'if that's what you want, darling.'

twenty-seven

Andrew had phoned almost every day. More often than not, Rosie had switched the call directly through to voicemail, and deleted his messages without even listening to them. Funny, she thought, that she always used to save the messages he left.

Eddie had kept her informed of the plan, too. Andrew had been cautious at first but, before long, messages addressed to 'Hot Honey' – the name that Hate-'em-all had come up with – were coming in thick and fast. Andrew was clearly an old hand at this, and even had a picture of 'Corky' – who was, apparently, a 13-year-old boy who was into films, music, and skateboarding. After receiving Corky's picture, Eddie asked a particular young-looking prostitute that he knew to pose naked for a photo. Computer Terry pixilated her face, and they'd sent it to Andrew, along with an invitation to visit her at home – 'when my parents will be out' – the same day he was flying back from Thailand.

The phone rang in Hewitt Way. There weren't many

people who called that number any more, so it was with some trepidation that Rosie picked up the receiver.

'Hello?'

'Where the *fuck* have you been?'

'I've been busy filming,' Rosie said, as casually as she could.

'What's up, Rosie?' Johnny said. He knew that tone too well. 'You sound upset.'

'No, no. I'm fine. I'm just tired.'

'You sure? Is Ruby okay?'

A million questions shot through Rosie's mind. Had Eddie spoken to him? Or Hate-'em-all? 'Ruby's fine,' she said, slowly. 'She's with Aunt Madge.'

'She still got that psycho dog?'

Rosie breathed a sign of relief... he didn't know.

'So... is my famous film-star wife too busy to come and see her husband then?'

'No, it's not that...' said Rosie. 'Look, filming's finished now – I would love to come and see you.' As she said the words, Rosie realised that not only was she prepared to visit him... she wanted to. 'I... I miss you.'

For a moment the line fell silent.

'Are you still there?' Rosie asked.

'Yeah, yeah, I'm still 'ere. I 'aint got much choice, have I?' Johnny said, with a laugh. 'When can I come?'

'When do you want to come? Tomorrow?'

'I haven't got a V.O.,' said Rosie. Anyone visiting HMP Maidstone needed a visiting order, and it always took a day or two to arrange it.

'There'll be one waiting for you at the gate,' said Johnny. 'I gotta go. My phone card's about to die on me.'

The line went dead. He was gone.

Taking a seat on the old sofa, Rosie was surprised at the emotions that she was feeling. The brief conversation with Johnny had been easy… *comforting*, even. She couldn't remember the last time she had taken any comfort from her husband, and the safety net that surrounded the Mullins family. Had she been too hard on Johnny? She *had* always looked down on him, that was true enough. But Johnny was a product of his environment – a tough, dog-eat-dog world.

She found herself thinking about their first date… she had been 17 when they first met, at that party he'd organised with Eddie for the cast of *EastEnders*. They had clicked immediately and, at the end of the night he'd invited her to his new club, the Manhattan, just off Commercial Road.

As a genuine East End girl, Rosie had heard a great deal about the club, and was so excited to be visiting it with one of its owners, no less. She'd made a real effort, preparing for their fist night out together – buying a little black dress from a designer boutique on the Roman Road that fitted the occasion perfectly, using heated rollers for her hair, putting on false eyelashes, make-up… the works.

When Rosie arrived at the club, it being a Saturday there was a long line of people waiting patiently to get inside. Rosie, as instructed, walked straight to the front where the doorman – a real oak of a man – took one look at her and asked, 'You Rosie?'

No sooner had she responded, he ushered her inside and, clearing a way through the sea of people, showed her to the VIP lounge at the back. Johnny was waiting for her, dressed in a tonic mohair suit, black python shoes, and a double-cuff, monogrammed shirt – looking like he just stepped off some yacht in Monte Carlo.

From that day on she had been under Johnny's wing – no more queuing to get into clubs, no more waiting at the bar, no more unwanted attention from any pushy geezers. She had respect.

After speaking to Rosie, Johnny made his way back to the cell with an unfamiliar lightness in his heart. Her sudden change of attitude had been a real surprise, but it was very welcome. Things were beginning to fall into place in Johnny's world – business was good and, quite out of the blue, it looked like reconciliation with his missus was on the cards. With hindsight, it must be difficult for her on the outside, he thought. *Maybe I was too hard on her.*

The change in him was obvious. Unlike Eddie, whose mood was almost impossible to read, Johnny's state of mind was always reflected in the way he carried himself. On the landing, as he passed a con he vaguely knew, he was surprised to hear him say, 'All right John?' On any other day, Johnny would have thought it a liberty, him being so familiar. But today he didn't care.

'Yeah,' he said, stopping. The con took a small step

backwards… he looked suddenly nervous. 'My missus is coming up tomorrow. She's finished filming.'

'Oh yeah? She was in that thing, wasn't she? I saw it in the paper,' said the con, beginning to relax. 'Perhaps we can have a word with the guv'nor. Maybe roll out the red carpet, eh?'

'Well, we'll see?' said Johnny, breaking a smile. 'See you later.'

As Johnny walked on, he heard the con ask, 'Oi, John. Can I get her autograph?'

'You'd be fucking lucky,' Johnny replied, not breaking his step.

The following morning, as the train made its way towards Maidstone, Rosie looked out at the Kent countryside. It was pouring down with rain and the sky was a mass of threatening, thick grey clouds. It looked as miserable as she felt.

She so desperately wanted to share the burden of guilt, to tell Johnny exactly what had happened… but she knew what he was like. If he found out – what with him in prison, unable to do anything about it – he would go insane. No, Rosie decided, telling Johnny what had happened to their daughter was completely out of the question.

The prison is directly opposite Maidstone West rail station so, when Rosie arrived, she was faced with the tall, oppressive walls that dominated the skyline. Walking over to the entrance, Rosie buried all of her feelings of anger and guilt and switched her focus firmly on the imminent visit. She couldn't let on that anything was wrong.

As Rosie went through the laborious security checks, she noticed that the prison officers were being unusually helpful and polite. She didn't know if this was down to her new-found fame, or whether it was that Johnny had the officers in his pocket, but it was certainly not something that she remembered ever happening before.

She took a seat at the designated table in the visitors' hall and quickly checked her appearance in a small compact mirror. Although she felt like crap, she didn't look too bad, she decided – her tired eyes were hidden behind a pair of large Dolce and Gabbana sunglasses.

Johnny finally arrived and, without a word, wrapped his muscular arms around her small frame in a strong embrace. Rosie stifled a sob.

'Now, now,' he said, still holding on tight. 'What's all this?'

Feeling the eyes of the other visitors on her, Rosie broke away, but not before kissing Johnny gently on the lips. They took their seats, and Johnny reached over and grabbed her hands.

'It's good to see you, Johnny,' she said.

'You too,' he said. After a moment's silence he asked the question that she knew was coming: 'What's going on, Rose? Why the sudden change?'

Rosie didn't reply – she just looked down at her lap. Johnny reached over and, with slow and deliberate movements, removed her sunglasses, folded in the arms, and placed them down on the table. Her eyes were red and puffy, surrounded by deep, dark circles. The pain was blatantly obvious. Johnny sat back in his chair.

'So, you gonna tell me, then?'

'Just a minute,' Rosie mumbled, getting up. He throat was dry... she could barely talk. She walked over to the canteen hatch and returned with two cups of tea.

'So you need a cuppa first? Fair enough,' he said. 'Well, now you've got tea, tell me what's wrong.'

'I'm okay, Johnny... really.'

'Do you want a divorce? Is that it?' he said. 'Because if you do...'

Rosie put down the plastic cup, took a deep breath, and held it. 'No. No, Johnny. I don't want a divorce. It's not that.' She proceeded to splutter through a range of lame excuses – that she was tired, she didn't want to be an actress anymore, she had been ill, that she missed him.

Although it might not have been one of her strongest performances, Johnny was no good with what he called 'all that lovey-dovey stuff', and was not the kind of person who felt comfortable talking about his feelings. Things to Johnny were either black or they were white. So, after a listening to ten minutes of Rosie going on about why she was feeling down, he decided to back off. Whether he believed her or whether he just chose not to pry, Rosie didn't know. But what was important was that his questions had ended. Still, for the remainder of the visit he didn't let go of her hand.

Ruby only briefly came up in the conversation. 'So how's our little girl?' Johnny had asked.

'Oh, she's good… you know,' Rosie said.

'It was nice to see her again, face-to-face. She was acting up a bit, y'know.'

'Well, she's almost a teenager now. That's what happens,' said Rosie, suddenly feeling a flash of self-loathing as she remembered that that was the same excuse that Andrew had given when Ruby started behaving strangely.

'I suppose so,' Johnny said. 'School okay?'

'Yeah, I think so.'

'Good.'

'Oh, I forgot to ask,' Rosie said, steering the conversation away from their daughter's state of mind. 'She wanted me to ask you something.'

'Oh yeah?'

'She wants a dog. A puppy.'

Johnny sneered. 'I don't know. They're a bit of an 'andful.'

'It might be good for her,' said Rosie. Thinking about it, she couldn't help but feel that a puppy might actually help Rube take her mind off what had happened to her.

'I suppose it would keep Hate-'em-all away from the house, if nothing else.'

Rosie laughed. She hadn't laughed for a long time. Looking at Johnny's face, she remembered what they had been like, at the beginning… before the drugs and the fights. He was a good man, in his heart. Not bad looking, either. Rosie caught herself imagining a reconciliation, with them living together again after his release, as a family, back in their little house on Hewitt Way.

Careful, Rosie, she said to herself. She had been so serious about Andrew and, even though their relationship was now in tatters, she was aware that she was, in a very strange way, still 'on the rebound'. She'd tried so hard in the past to get away from Johnny – did she really want to just fall back into his arms, get sucked back into his world?

At that moment Rosie felt very alone. Her attempt at fitting in to the so-called 'respectable' world had ended in disaster... and Johnny's world – although familiar – was a violent, unpleasant place to live. She was beginning to regret calling Eddie and getting him involved. Sure, Andrew deserved all that was coming to him, but she didn't really believe in handing the responsibility of the punishment over to Eddie. By calling him, she had handed control over to him... and that was a frightening thought.

The buzzer went, snapping Rosie out of her thoughts and signalling the end of their time together. They said their goodbyes and Rosie watched as Johnny walked back to the security gates. She turned, and headed for the exit.

'Rose!' Johnny's voice echoed from the other end of the visiting hall.

'What?'

'Tell Ruby I said yes,' he said. 'She can have that puppy. Tell her Daddy said it's okay.'

twenty-eight

A Starbucks coffee shop was hardly Eddie or Hate-'em-all's natural habitat, so Rosie was surprised when she received a call telling her to meet them there. They were already there, sipping huge mugs of coffee and devouring pastries, when Rosie arrived. She was surprised to find the café almost empty. She checked her watch. Although they were in those 'dead' hours – when the shoppers had gone home and anyone out for a night on the town had yet to hit town – Rosie suspected that the sight of these two gorillas sitting in the window might have deterred many potential customers. Eddie was talking on his mobile phone and, on seeing Rosie, waved her over. Hate-'em-all fetched her a latte and a lemon bun, and they all moved to a larger table in the corner, where Eddie opened his laptop.

Andrew was due back from Thailand in two days' time, and Eddie wanted to know every last detail about his return – the time his flight landed at Heathrow, the make, model and registration of his car, everything. Eddie was meticulous in everything he did – that was just the way he liked to do business.

'When did you last speak to him?' Eddie asked.

'Yesterday, after I left Maidstone.'

'And?'

'He said that he missed me.'

'Sick *bastard*,' muttered Hate-'em-all.

'I said I was going to meet him in town for a special dinner when he got back… for his birthday.' In fact, it had been very difficult speaking to Andrew, still pretending that she loved him. Rosie knew she had to be cool, she had to box clever.

'He won't go home first, then? Before he drives out to Epping?'

'His flight lands just after four in the afternoon. I said we'd meet in town at six-thirty. So even if doesn't go to Epping, he might nip into the office first, but he won't have time to go home.'

'He'd better not,' said Eddie, 'if he goes back home, and realises you've fucked off, he'll smell a rat.'

'I don't know, there are a lot of "ifs",' said Rosie. 'Maybe we should forget it… call the police.'

'He'll come, trust me,' said Harry, opening up a webpage on the laptop. 'He's been sending messages every five minutes, he has. Listen to this… "Cool, see you at seven. I ride my bike over. Can't wait to see you". Then he says –'

A young couple sat down at the table next to them and,

in perfect union, Eddie and Hate-'em-all slowly turned their heads. They couple glanced over, the young man uttered a hurried 'sorry', and they made their way to sit elsewhere.

'Go on then,' said Eddie, after the couple had moved.

'Well, he checked that the parents wouldn't be in, that's all. I said they were in Corfu.'

'Right,' said Eddie, after finishing the last dregs of his coffee, 'let's go.' He stood up, and Hate-'em-all put away the laptop.

'So what happens now? I don't have to be there, do I?'

'That's up to you. But I do need you to identify his car. I'll pick you up at Hewitt Way on Sunday, one-thirty.' He leant over Rosie, and added, 'Make sure you're there.'

'I'll be there.'

Sunday afternoon, and the baggage reclaim at the arrival lounge at Heathrow was crowded with holidaymakers, businessmen, backpackers and other travellers, all huddled around the slow-moving carousels. Andrew Brook-Fields spotted his black, hard-shell suitcase approaching, and heaved it onto his trolley. He looked at his watch – 4.27. He hurried down the green, 'Nothing to Declare' channel , and past the lines of chauffeurs and families waiting in the arrivals hall beyond.

Before heading out to the car park, he felt inside his jacket pocket and removed a small piece of paper. Opening it, he smiled – he still had the address, safe and sound. Not that he needed to write it down. He had memorised it.

As he strolled over to the car he took out his mobile phone, switched it on, and tapped in a text message. Seconds after sending it, a sound made him stop dead. He could have sworn that he'd heard a familiar beeping sound. He looked around the cold, still floor of the multi-storey… there was nobody in the vicinity.

When Rosie's phone had alerted her about the incoming text, she had instinctively shrunk back down into her seat. She had been waiting in the car park for over half-an-hour with Eddie, and that didn't include the 45 minutes that they had spent driving around, looking for Andrew's black Range Rover. Eddie had borrowed an old car from a 'business associate', deciding that his Merc was rather conspicuous, and had been furious that it didn't have a CD player for his 'Greatest Arias' compilation album.

'What?' Eddie whispered, watching Andrew unlock the door and climb inside his car. 'What did he say?'

Rosie read the message: 'Flight diverted – stuck in bloody Poland for few hours! Won't make dinner – so sorry. Make it up to you when I get home x.' *God*, Rosie thought, *those lies come easy*.

'He's going for it,' she said.

Andrew started his engine and began to ease out of the parking space.

'Right,' said Eddie, 'Get out. I'll call you later. You can even come along, if you like.'

'You know I'm not going to do that, don't you?'

Rosie eased open the door and, keeping her head down, ducked into the doorway of the car park's stairwell.

She watched as Andrew's car drove round towards the ramp to the floor below and, once it had turned the corner, Eddie started the engine.

Keeping a two-car distance, Eddie followed the Range Rover out of the airport and onto the motorway. He picked up his mobile, called Hate-'em-all, and said, 'We're leaving now', and hung up.

Johnny had been true to his word and, no sooner had Rosie arrived back from the visit, than there was a delivery, by hand, of £2,000 in cash for Ruby's puppy. The next morning, accompanied by Aunt Madge and Stevie, they had gone to a specialist pet shop near Brixton, where Ruby had chosen a ten-week-old, blue merle, teacup Chihuahua… an adorable little animal with an apple-shaped head and a short, wide nose. She might have been 'a bit Paris Hilton' for Aunt Madge, but for Ruby it was love at first sight. She named her 'Sugar'.

Ruby went to stay a few more nights at Aunt Madge's, 'so Sugar and Dibble can make friends', and the two of them filled their days with doggie-talk. As Andrew's return grew nearer, Rosie had a lot on her mind… but not so much that she didn't notice that Ruby seemed to be slowly recovering. They never spoke about Andrew, not even mentioning his name.

Rosie always called on her Aunt Madge whenever there was a crisis in her life – and she'd had her fair share – so, after leaving Eddie at Heathrow, she got the express train back to London and went straight to Britley House.

twenty-nine

It was a typically cold November evening as Andrew drove along the M25, heading towards his destination in Essex. As the skies blackened, he switched on the windscreen wipers and fiddled with the radio, finally settling on a classical music station.

Once he was off the motorway, heading deeper and deeper into the Essex countryside, Andrew leaned forward, peering through the rain that was now drumming on the windscreen. Eventually his sat-nav announced, 'You have arrived at your destination.'

After turning off the lights and engine, Andrew sat quite still for a good three minutes. His heart was racing as he stepped out of the car and headed over towards the secluded bungalow. The surrounding gardens with their adjoining fields and woodland were growing dim as the evening light faded. One solitary light shone from inside, and there were no cars parked in the drive.

Gingerly making his way up the narrow brick path, he

noticed that the front door was slightly open. For a second he stood silently, listening. He could hear the slightly muffled sound of music… young music… teenage music. He smiled. After tapping gently on the door, he cautiously stepped inside.

'Hiya,' he called, hesitantly. 'Anyone home?'

No reply… just the distant sound of pop music.

'You hoo,' he called, stepping into the hallway. He looked around… something wasn't quite right.

'Hello?'

At that moment, a figure stepped out in front of Andrew. In the darkness, he could only make out the silhouette… it was a man, a big man. Andrew turned and, through the half-open front door saw a car speed up to the bungalow. It skidded to a halt and another large man jumped out. Before he knew what was happening, the man in the hallway had grabbed him in a tight bear hug.

'What is this?' he bleated. 'Get off me!'

Eddie rushed into the hall and slipped a black hood over Andrew's head. They dragged him, kicking and screaming, into the bungalow's lounge. He was dumped into a chair – his attempt to stand up swiftly foiled by a hard punch to his right eye. He heard the sound of gaffer tape being torn off its roll, and then felt rough hands binding his hands and feet to a chair. The hood was then pulled off. There in front of him stood two men who had had never seen before in his life.

'Who are you?' he asked, his breathing already frantic. 'What do you want?'

'I've got some bad news,' said Eddie. '"Hot Honey" can't make it.'

'What?' Andrew cried.

'It's a shame, because I'm sure she was *dying* to meet the young lad she'd been talking to.'

'Please... I don't know what you're talking about!' Andrew's eyes were very wide. 'Who are you?'

Hate-'em-all stepped forward and pinched Andrew's cheeks.

'Evening Corky,' he said.

Ruby was safely out of earshot, playing with Sugar in her bedroom, and Aunt Madge led Rosie through to make some tea. Her homely little kitchen always looked exactly the same – two damp tea-towels were casually draped over the cutlery tray and, on the draining board, a haphazard jumble of pots, pans and crockery. Aunt Madge picked up Dibble's water bowl from the kitchen floor and filled it from the tap.

'Aunt Madge,' Rosie said, switching on the kettle, 'did I do the right thing?'

She didn't reply – it was a rhetorical question and they both knew the answer. What Andrew had done to Ruby – and God knows how many other little girls – was so repugnant that Rosie's instinctive, knee-jerk reaction was to dish out the most brutal revenge imaginable. What mother or self-respecting person wouldn't? But, now she was thinking more rationally, she regretted going to Eddie. Of course, the very fact that she *had* told Eddie made it impossible to go through the official channels. Eddie was colder, more calculating, more rational than Johnny had ever been… that must, subconsciously, be why she went to him, she thought. But now, at the same moment that she was waiting for the kettle to boil, she knew that Andrew was driving towards certain death. And it wouldn't be quick. Did she really want his blood on her hands?

'I'm not going soft, am I?' Rosie asked. 'It's just…' Her words tailed off.

After some thought, Aunt Madge calmly said, 'I know you're not going soft, Rose.'

'When I found out just what Andrew had done, calling Eddie seemed like the only thing to do.'

'And now you're beginning to wish you hadn't?'

'But what could I do? If I went to the law, it would be all over the papers. Then Johnny would have read it, and… well, God only knows what would have happened.'

'I know,' said Madge. 'He would've gone after Andrew, then Andrew's family… then you. Then me, I expect. He wouldn't stop until he'd destroyed the whole world.'

'Including himself,' said Rosie.

'Besides, with the police, what would happen? Andrew would be just like any other paedophile – sex offenders' register, most probably given a three-year community order, some programme or other. He deserves worse than that, love.'

Rosie dropped two teabags into the teapot and shuddered. 'Oh my God, what am I doing?' She started to cry. 'Of course I want revenge. You know, beat him up a bit, cut his ears off... don't stop at just his ears. He deserves it for what he did. But if I don't stop them, I'll be responsible for a man being...' she lowered her voice, '...tortured. *Murdered.* I don't think I can live with that.'

Rosie wiped away her tears – she had to think clearly. The decisions she made over the next couple of hours would affect many people's lives... including poor Ruby's. If she didn't stop Eddie and Hate-'em-all, she'd be beholden to them – which would mean beholden to Johnny, too – for ever. It would be back to trudging around the country on prison visits, year after year. She'd be made to throw away her acting career too, which meant no more financial independence for her, Aunt Madge, or Ruby. And, to top it off, she would be guilty of murder... maybe not directly, but guilty all the same.

At that moment, in Aunt Madge's cluttered kitchen, sipping Yorkshire tea, Rosie felt like her whole life had come crashing down around her.

'Well,' Aunt Madge said, 'it's your decision.'

'I know.'

'Whatever you decide to do, Stevie and me will back you up, one hundred percent.'

Rosie looked over at Madge. 'I've got to find a way to call them off,' she said. 'I've got to try.'

Just one look at Andrew, and Eddie knew that he hadn't the first clue who he and Hate-'em-all were or why they were there.

'What do you want? Money?' When they didn't reply, he raised his voice, adopting a superior tone… or the closest he could manage. 'Who are you? If you're the police, I want to see identification. I know my rights.'

Andrew watched as Hate-'em-all walked over to a desk in one corner of the room and turned off the pop music that was still playing on the stereo. It was then that he spotted his laptop. It was open and displayed on the screen was a slow slideshow of popular backgrounds – water lilies, the Grand Canyon, Stonehenge…

Taking in the rest of the room, Andrew saw that the curtains were tightly drawn and the lightbulb was dim, so his surroundings were not immediately obvious. In another corner was a single bed with a bare mattress. His heart froze when he saw the pairs of handcuffs hanging from each corner of the metal bed frame. After rocking to and fro, pulling at his binds, he let his head drop. Immediately, he wished he hadn't –underneath his feet, surrounding the chair, the floor was covered with a thick blue plastic sheet.

There was no way that this was the police.

'Let me go,' he said, wriggling with frantic energy. 'Let me go now.'

Hate-'em-all stared back at him with eyes devoid of sympathy. Realising that he was in no position to be giving out orders, Andrew tried again.

'Please, please…' he begged, his voice changing from one in authority to one pleading for his life. 'I've got money.'

Eddie moved towards him, very slowly, causing Andrew to flinch. He slipped the black hood back over Andrew's head, then he and Hate-'em-all left the room.

'If it's money you want, I've got plenty,' Andrew cried. 'Where are you going.'

'I've got to make a phone call. Don't go anywhere, all right?' said Eddie, and left.

thirty

'Look, look Mum! Ain't she sweet? *Sit*, Sugar. Sit!'

Rosie smiled a half smile but she wasn't really listening. Sitting on the chair in front of the gas fire she checked her mobile every minute, desperate to know what was going on in that little bungalow by Epping Forest. Now that she had made the decision to unleash Eddie and Hate-'em-all Harry on Andrew, she was faced with a serious problem: if they did manage to grab him – and Rosie was convinced that they had done that already – what could she do to stop them? True, she still had a copy of the security tapes from the Keyhole Club, but she'd already played that card. By telling Eddie what Andrew had done, she had started an avalanche. She knew that Eddie blamed her for everything. *She* was the one who had deceived Johnny and taken Ruby to live with a paedophile. Eddie was an evil, threatening figure at the best of times, but now he had this terrible hold on her. With this control, she would never be free of him.

But what could she do? If Johnny found out he would most likely kill her for lying to him, for mugging him off... for putting Ruby at risk. The only option she could think of was going to Florida with Stevie. But that was just a pipedream – the Mullins brothers would find her, eventually.

The text alert from her mobile almost made her heart stop. She opened the message immediately – 'The fish is on the hook'. No longer could she pretend that, by some miracle, Andrew had escaped from their trap. They had him.

Rosie paled and looked over at Aunt Madge, her eyes full of fear, panic, and desperation.

'What's wrong, Mummy?' asked Ruby, looking up at her.

'Nothing, sweetheart. Mummy's okay,' she said, rubbing her eyes and getting to her feet.

'Come on,' said Aunt Madge, 'let's put the kettle on.'

Rosie followed her into the cluttered kitchen, closing the door behind her. Ruby picked up her puppy and started to stroke her affectionately. Through the door she could hear sobbing. She couldn't make out what they were saying – apart from a 'No... no' from Rosie and Aunt Madge mumbling reassuringly.

Ten minutes later Rosie emerged, dabbing her eyes and gently blowing her nose. She picked up her keys, slipped her phone into her pocket, and pulled on her coat. Then, without saying a word, she kissed Ruby on the forehead and hugged Aunt Madge, holding the embrace for a fraction longer than usual.

Closing the front door behind her, Rosie hurried along the concrete landing and into the night. Ducking her head and pulling her collar up to guard against the chill wind, she made her way to her car. She felt so nervous that, as she fumbled to unlock the door, she dropped the car keys. Picking them up, she looked up at a break in the clouds and caught a glimpse of the full moon emerging. She sighed; what she was going to do would change everything. She had to be strong… she had to be brave.

An unexpected sense of calm came over her as she drove through the dark, wet streets of East London, regularly checking the rear view mirror. She might not have planned to confront Andrew but, now that she was going to, she relished the thought of it. Keeping one eye on the road, she pulled out her mobile and scrolled down to Eddie's name in her list of contacts.

'Eddie, it's me. I've decided, I coming over.'

'You what?'

'I want to see him. I won't be long.'

As she hung up, she look back at the rear view mirror. Nothing. Were the police still following her? Could she really be sure that 'Harris' was a policeman anyway? *Typical*, she thought.

Rosie had experienced enough recently to know that things rarely went according to plan.

thirty-one

Under the black hood, Andrew's eyes bulged like he'd taken an ounce of whizz. But there was no need for artificial stimulation... this high was due to shock and adrenalin, nothing else. The room had been largely silent for what seemed to him like hours. Whenever the occasional hoot of an owl or a scream of a fox penetrated the walls of the bungalow, his heart would stop... then resume its frantic, unstable rhythm. There was a tightness at the back of his throat, choking the blood to his brain. His mind was clogged with questions, but they were all eclipsed by the biggest of them... one he kept asking himself over and over again: *Am I going to die?*

After several wrong turnings, Rosie finally pulled up outside the isolated bungalow. She was surprised to find the front door unlocked, and cautiously made her way inside. Eddie and Hate-'em-all were waiting in the kitchen, bent over a table snorting cocaine. It was obvious from the frenzied look in their eyes that these were not the first lines of the evening.

'About fucking time! What did you do, walk?' Eddie said, with a sneer. 'Well, we've got your loverboy, you slag. Now we're going to clean up your mess.'

Rosie glanced at Hate-'em-all. In a strange sort of way, she had always liked him. He might have been from the same mould as Eddie and Johnny, but he had some redeeming qualities. He'd always treated Rosie with respect, and she'd never heard him raise his voice, curse or be uncouth. But she wasn't unfamiliar with his other side, either – the one that earned him his nickname. Maybe he had that violent streak because of something specific that had happened to him during his formative years – an underlying problem. Or maybe there was no explanation other than Hate-'em-all-Harry simply enjoyed inflicting pain. Staring at his wide, black pupils and dead smile, Rosie knew immediately that if she was looking for an ally, she wouldn't find one in him.

'Can I see him? Alone?'

'Through there,' said Eddie, gesturing towards the sitting room.

Rosie wanted her moment with Andrew. She wanted – no, *needed* – to know what made an intelligent, affluent, middle-aged man do the heinous things he had done.

Stepping into the room it was as if she was physically pushed backwards. Everything about the place screamed at her to leave – the sight of a hooded man, bound and shaking, the acidic smell of fear hanging in the air like thick mist. She recognised Andrew's computer on a desk in the corner, and noticed a bed. She instantly knew why

Eddie had put that there. Rosie took a deep breath and moved forward. Hearing footsteps, Andrew looked up.

'Please…' came the muffled voice, 'please…'

The sound he made was weak, pitiful. Rosie noticed a dark stain on the front of his trousers – he had wet himself. She leaned forward, took hold of the top of the hood and slipped it off his head. Andrew's pupils shrank as the light hit them… then grew as he saw who it was.

'Rosie! Oh, thank god.'

The last time she had looked into those eyes, there had been a softness, full of what she thought was love. That was now replaced with fear. Thinking back, she realised that they never really had *anything* in common. But still, blinded by love, she had fallen for his smooth words and thin veneer of respectability. She had been a fool.

'Why?' she whispered. She had rehearsed the questions in the car… but now, face to face with him, she could only manage this three-letter word.

'Why?' said Andrew, clinging tightly to the pretence and shaking his head. 'Why, what? Who are these men? What's going on, darling?'

Rosie flinched. 'Don't darling me, you bastard!' At that moment, the dam holding back her feelings broke. 'I *trusted* you. How could you do that to Ruby?'

'No, no! You've got it all wrong.'

Rosie walked over to the laptop and opened a file of images. The photos of Ruby began to flash across the screen.

'Is that what this is all about?' Andrew blinked and forced out an unconvincing laugh. 'Pictures!'

Within seconds, a sharp slap whipped hard across his face.

'I know what you did, Andrew. Ruby told me.'

'You don't understand,' he yelled. 'She's lying! It was her, she wanted me to…'

Instinctively lifting her hands to her ears to block out the lies, Rosie screamed: 'She's a *child*! She's *twelve years old*! An innocent *child*.'

Returning to the laptop, Rosie deleted the images of Ruby – she never wanted to see those again – and opened another file of pictures. Watching the stream of his sickening souvenirs of years of abuse of children, Andrew was no longer able to protest his innocence. His head drooped towards the floor.

'Turn it off,' he murmured, 'please.'

'This why you go to Thailand. You *pig*!' Rosie screamed. 'You think I'm just a common little trollop that you picked up from the gutter. Someone you could take advantage of. Then, when you got bored of me, you went after my daughter.'

'It's not like that,' he whined.

'What you did,' said Rosie, almost drunk with rage, 'is worse than murder. You're worse than an *animal*. It flies in the face of natural instincts. You think I'm so stupid that you could get away with it?'

'Please! Listen to me!'

'No, *you* listen to *me*,' Rosie said. 'I can't stop what's going to happen, even if I wanted to.'

'Who are those men?' Andrew was unnervingly still.

'Eddie Mullins, my brother-in-law… my husband's twin brother, Ruby's uncle. And Harry, Ruby's godfather.'

'Oh, Jesus…' muttered Andrew. Finally, the pieces had fallen into place. 'Please, you have to help me. Listen to me, I –'

'Help you?' Rosie exclaimed, in a voice halfway between a scream and hysterical laugh. 'Did you listen to my daughter when you… *raped* her? You fucking *animal*!'

'Please, Rosie… *please* help me,' Andrew pleaded. 'Look, I *know* you. You're a good person.'

Rosie walked to the door and, after composing herself, turned to him again. 'What's going to happen to you, Andrew… I don't want you to get it confused with revenge. It's not. It's about justice… for Ruby. Goodbye, Andrew.'

'No!' he screamed, 'Wait! Wait!'

As soon as Rosie had left, Eddie and Hate-'em-all entered.

'This ain't no courtroom. We're judge, jury and prosecutor, and we've found you guilty,' said Eddie. Noticing the laptop, still running the slideshow, he told Harry: 'Shut that sick shit off, will you?'

'Please, let me just…' Andrew's now timid voice tailed off.

'I'm not triumphant in what I'm about to do,' Eddie continued. 'I feel no remorse, no anger.' He took a breath before continuing. 'I sentence you to death, and I'm going to tell you why.'

'Please… please…'

'There is a line, Mr Brook-Fields. No one can see it, but everyone knows it's there. And when you took a young girl – a twelve-year-old little girl – you took away her innocence, you crossed that line.' Andrew's sobs intensified as Eddie went on: 'I'm not a yob or a common killer, I'm a technician. I enjoy my job. You're an intelligent man, been around the block. Do you know what's inscribed in stone outside the Old Bailey? Do you?'

'Well, answer him!' said Harry, landing a hard blow directly on the bridge of Andrew's nose. It made a dull cracking sound.

'No!' screamed Andrew, blood beginning to seep from his nostrils.

'Well, I'm going to tell you. It says "Defend the children of the poor and punish the wrongdoer." Did you know that? "Defend the children of the poor and punish the wrongdoer." And that's why we're here – to punish the wrongdoer.'

Hate-'em-all removed his jacket, unclipped his gold cufflinks and slowly rolled up his double-cuffed shirtsleeves. Meanwhile, Eddie put a CD into the stereo and pressed 'play'. The opening bars of Pavarotti's performance of Nessun Dorma filled the room.

'You'll like this, being an educated man,' Eddie said, turning up the volume to a deafening level. He took off his jacket then slowly unbuttoned and removed his crisp, white shirt. Next, he let his trousers fall and, after carefully pinching the creases together, placed them over the back of the chair.

Harry cut a thick line of cocaine on the desk by the laptop, and Eddie, now in just his boxer shorts and socks, bent over and vacuumed it up with a loud, prolonged sniff. As he did so, Andrew caught sight of the formidable Celtic cross and the name 'Johnny' tattooed on Eddie's broad, hairy back.

'Look… Eddie, isn't it? Eddie, I'm not a monster. You've got it all wrong,' he shouted over the blaring music, which was reaching its climax.

Hate-'em-all did a line himself as Eddie opened a lock knife with a three-inch blade. He cut through the gaffer tape holding Andrew's legs.

'No, stop… please!' screamed Andrew, as his trousers were pulled off him.

The track ended, and, just as Puccini's O soave fanciulla started to play, Eddie looked up at him and said, 'The time for talking is over, Andrew. You are now in the teeth of the devil, and God help you.'

Sitting in the car outside, Rosie could hear frantic shouts and screams drowning the beautiful sound of Pavarotti's voice. When the music changed, she recognised the melody instantly – it was from La Bohème, the opera she had been to see with Andrew. She looked over at the bungalow… she knew what Eddie and Hate-'em-all were doing to Andrew. They were taking turns at him.

Rosie started the engine of the car and pulled away. She hadn't driven more than a few hundred yards when she turned into a lay-by.

'Oh my god,' she muttered, clutching the steering wheel as tightly as she could. She looked down at the clock on the dashboard. Andrew revolted and disgusted Rosie. He might even have been evil, but Rosie knew that if something didn't happen soon, she'd be responsible for taking Andrew's life, and didn't that make her equally as evil? She stared out at the country road, weighing the anger and resentment she felt against his life.

'Where are you?' she said, out loud.

She slotted the gear stick into first and gunned the engine. As the car reached the end of the lane she slowed down to a crawl. An unusual feeling washed over her... a strange mixture of horror and relief.

Parked either side of the narrow road were no less than six police cars, and a menacing armoured truck, its windows shielded by metal cages. More than a dozen armed policemen – elite specialist firearms officers, carrying MP5 machine guns, Glock 19s and Tazers, and dressed in black overalls, body armour, bullet-proof vests and helmets, were on stand-by ready and waiting to climb into the vehicles. A few of them raised their weapons when they saw Rosie's car approaching.

'Easy,' came a familiar voice, and the guns pointed at Rosie were slowly lowered.

She looked over and instantly recognised the man sitting inside one of the cars: it was 'Harris'. Their eyes locked as Rosie pulled up alongside him, and slowly wound down her window. For a moment they just stared at each other.

'Are you following me?' she eventually said, with a slight smile.

'What makes you think that,' 'Harris' replied. 'No, Mrs Mullins, *not you*. But we are about to close in on your family, as a matter of fact. The boys have been naughty again… very naughty. They've been shifting some serious amounts of cocaine recently.'

'Cocaine?' Rosie muttered. It was no real surprise that they had been up to their old tricks again. That was who they were.

'Yes, cocaine,' he said. 'We've been watching Eddie's office for quite some time now, in fact. Sharon, his secretary, is actually an undercover WPC.'

Rosie stared defiantly at 'Harris' before speaking again.

'So,' she said, 'are you going to nick me, or what?'

'No, Mrs Mullins. We'll need to talk to you, of course. Take a statement. But that can wait.'

Rosie's mind was racing. As the police had been following her for a while now, they would, at least, know that she was not involved in the drug trafficking… but what they were about to discover at the bungalow would be far more than they were looking for.

'So I'm free to go?'

'Harris' nodded. 'Don't worry,' he said, as he started his engine, 'we know where to find you.'

Seconds later, the convoy of blue-and-white cars was speeding towards the bungalow.

Rosie knew Eddie and Hate-'em-all would go down for

a very long stretch. With kidnapping, GBH and sexual assault added to the drugs charges, that would add up to a lot of years. And as for Andrew, there was enough evidence on that laptop for him to be removed from society for a long time – one less paedophile on the streets. He wouldn't easily forget the punishment doled out by Eddie and Hate-'em-all, either.

And what about her? What about Rosie Mullins? She had done something that was taboo in the underworld – she'd betrayed the Mullins name. If that was discovered, it would never be forgiven. Or forgotten. The Police might have *followed* her to the scene of the crime, but that was just a detail. Johnny and Eddie didn't worry about details. They would see it as the ultimate betrayal… would they ever forgive her?

But Rosie could worry about that tomorrow. For the moment at least, she was free. Free from them all.

And that was something.